A THOUSAND REASONS NOT TO RUN

TRISH TAYLOR

A Thousand Reasons Not to Run

Copyright © 2021 by Trish Taylor

First published in the United States 2021

All rights reserved

This is a work of fiction, names, characters, businesses, places, events, locales, and incidents are either products of the author's imagination or used in a fictitious manner. Any resemblance to actual persons, living or dead, or actual events is purely coincidental.

Credits
Book Cover Design
Vanessa Mendozzi

Editing
Kath Nyborg Storylogic LLC

ISBN: 978-1-7328655-6-3

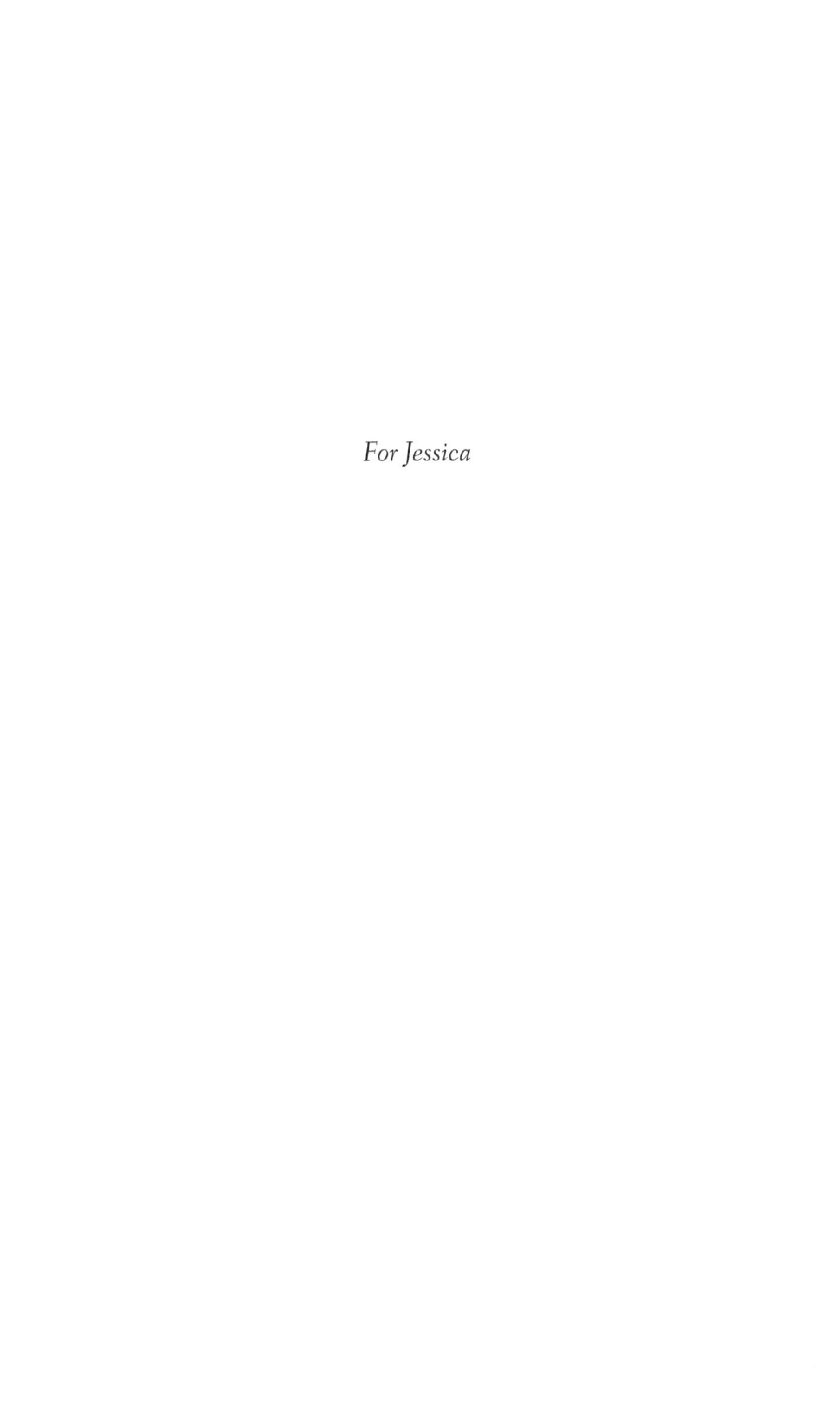

For Jessica

1

———

For once, Lexi wasn't thinking about all the things that could go wrong. She'd spent the morning deep in her research for a demanding client, and had allowed for a moment of reflection to enjoy the view over the bayou. The late September sun would still be warm for a few more weeks. She found the summers a little too hot here in the south, but as they drifted into fall and the humidity diminished, it was almost perfect.

Suddenly she was jolted from her thoughts. The sounds of the Volt's café, Tea and Two were normally the clink of teacups, or an occasional outburst after a dropped dish. Today there was a commotion. Lexi looked up to see a man in disarray, his sweating red face, bulging eyes and a shirt unbuttoned almost to his waist.

"They are coming to get me; you've got to help me."

Customers who but a moment ago were sipping coffee and reading newspapers were now all eyes on the man. He let out a scream that Lexi had only ever heard from those waking from nightmares of trauma, a mixture of memories stirred. She felt a surge of compassion for the man. The scream changed to a pitiful sobbing as he threw himself to the floor in the corner to curl into a ball.

The cute, floppy-haired guy, Zander, stopped grinding coffee and appeared from behind the counter. "It's okay, we won't let them get you."

The distressed man became calmer as Zander helped him up from the floor and led him to a table where he brought him a warm drink and chatted to him for a while. The coffee guy had some people skills. Zander was the manager of the Orwell themed cafe—Tea and Two Slices. Lexi had chatted with him a few times, and he seemed like a good guy.

A team member from the Harbor arrived and the man, now considerably calmer, left with him. Lexi hoped he would be okay and was glad that Zander had been there to help. The Harbor was another of the Volt's services. Its facility helped those who were experiencing homelessness, many were also struggling with substance abuse issues and mental health concerns.

The Volt served the community in so many positive ways; it reminded Lexi of The Sanctuary—the therapeutic facility where she grew up. It had in common a community garden, though the Volt's Eden was not as well-resourced as The Sanctuary's lush gardens. Though Lexi mainly stayed in the café or library to do her work, she sometimes wandered through the Atrium that connected all the different areas. She enjoyed the abundance of light and the feeling of peace. By design, there was no business carried out there. It was purely focused on recreation and relaxation, offering occasional yoga classes, tabletop games or simply a place to sit and enjoy the quiet. Members of the entrepreneurial center who tried to arrange business meetings in the Atrium were firmly reminded it was not a place for hustle.

Zander appeared and began wiping down tables. Lexi

asked. "Was he alright? You seemed to know what you were doing there."

Zander smiled as he refilled a napkin holder on an adjacent table. "On days like today, I'm grateful that all Volt staff members are trained in de-escalation techniques. It means encounters rarely intensify into anything dangerous."

"I don't know, it seemed like it came natural to you. I'm not prying, it's just the first time I've experienced anything other than peace and quiet, it's why I like to work here." Lexi suddenly worried she sounded like she was complaining about the noise. This is why she didn't make small talk; it was easy to get it wrong. "I just hope he's okay, he looked pretty scared for a while."

Zander smiled. "It's what this place is all about, being there for each other. He will be fine. He's new, he just lost his way for a minute."

Lexi realized that she liked Tea and Two because she was among people, even though she had no desire to get any closer than a table away. Lorna, her therapist, would approve—as a first step, at least. Lexi had been living in Tribune for almost two years and would probably make it her home. She was tired of moving around and had all she needed here. The Volt had become her oasis. It was far more than the community center she first believed it to be when she arrived for the race meeting that Lorna had inadvertently strong-armed her into. It was part of a deal, Lexi had to agree to it if she wanted to continue therapy.

Less than a year ago, things looked less positive. Her therapy had stalled. She had been unable to stop focusing on thoughts about the man she thought of as Doctor Death. Lorna had given her a prescription. Not a happy pill like Lexi wanted, but a different kind of remedy. "I'm going to prescribe some friendship for you. The delivery system will be your choice."

Lexi didn't want to work with anyone else, so agreed to listen to the mandatory treatment plan. Lorna handed Lexi a printed list, a single sheet with ten activities, groups and events, it was organized with information on commitment level and number of participants.

"Who even prints anymore?" Lexi had asked. She was feeling defensive even before she had looked at the paper. "You could have emailed it."

"Pick one or two and join. That's it. I don't want to hear from you until you can report back on how much fun you are having."

Lexi dreaded seeing what was on the list. But Lorna had handpicked activities Lexi would, if not enjoy, at least not poke her eyes out to avoid. Except for the belly dancing. Lexi still hadn't figured out if it was ironic or a way to make the other options appear more palatable. The running group was her preferred option, it required little commitment to "friendship." She hoped she could join and show up to the runs and leave straight after without feeling forced to socialize.

The running group's registration session was held at Tea and Two, that she would always be grateful for. She smiled, thinking of how Lorna's plan had almost worked. The coffee guy was smiling at her. She'd been looking in his direction while staring into space. He thought she was smiling at him. Oh God, she hoped she hadn't also been thinking out loud; she'd been talking to herself more frequently recently. It seemed the only way she could clarify her thoughts if she was without a notepad or device.

Zander asked, "Can I get you anything else?"

Lexi smiled and shook her head. Phew, he thought she was looking for a coffee refill. She would hate him to think she was flirting, no matter how cute he was. She couldn't risk making it awkward to be here, it was one of the only places she felt comfortable. Tribune was a pretty town, though other than the scenery and the Volt, it had little else going for it. Lorna was part of the reason Lexi had come to the area. It wasn't far from the tragedy that led her to live at The Sanctuary. Lorna, was the primary therapist and had treated Lexi for the whole of her time there. When Lorna decided to focus on private practice at her home in Tribune. Lexi decided it was as good a place as the next to start again. As far as she knew, no one remembered her or her story. When she told Lorna of her plans, she had given Lexi one of her looks and said, "Lifetime client moves closer to therapist. Nope, not creepy at all."

Lexi had been daydreaming for too long. She needed to continue her research, she headed to the library.

$$2$$

Though much of what Lexi needed could be found online, for in-depth details about local history or news stories there was a ton of resources that she could access offline and stay focused. Though she could find some useful information on research sites, even social media like Glass Jelly, it was hard to sift out the opinions from the facts. She was proud of her meticulous work and grateful for the library that was almost as well equipped as the one she used in college.

When she arrived today, she immediately felt that something wasn't right. The normally relaxed atmosphere around the library reception desk was missing. The vibe was hushed, but not in the sense you would expect. Victoria—the always helpful and enthusiastic clerk—was close to tears. Lexi was uncomfortable around overt displays of emotion. She didn't know what to do. She didn't feel like asking if she could use a meeting room as she'd planned. Before she had chance to think, Victoria approached her.

"You're the researcher, right?"

"Yes, why?"

Do you have a few minutes?" the clerk gestured towards a room behind the desk.

"I don't think so. I have work to do." Acutely uncomfortable, Lexi began to walk away.

Victoria followed her and lowered her voice. "I know you care about the library and the Volt. You wouldn't want to lose it, right? You need to hear what I have to say."

Lexi cared more than they could imagine. If something was threatening the library, she needed to know. She allowed the woman to lead her into the media room that overlooked the reception desk, Lexi thought she seemed paranoid, she was looking around and speaking in hushed tones.

"They are talking about closing the library."

"Who is talking about closing the library? Why?" Lexi asked. "That doesn't make sense."

"Money. What else? It's always money. The council say it's too expensive to run, especially here on the waterfront. But there's more going on. I think the whole Volt could be in danger."

Lexi wasn't expecting this and allowed Victoria to continue.

"They've been trying to get rid of the Harbor since it opened. The mayor has never accepted that those experiencing homelessness deserve to be part of the Volt or even the town. I wouldn't be surprised if they are gone before we are."

Lexi didn't see how she could help. She asked, "There's nothing official yet right, no firm plans it's just stuff being considered?"

Victoria sighed. "You've not been here long enough to see how it works. It always starts with a rumor, denials, but before long you realize the stuff that the powers-that-be claim won't happen, always does in the end. This place, once they take a part of it, it won't be long before it's all gone. If there is anything you can do, if you have any influence or know someone who has, please...."

With an imploring look Victoria went back to her station behind the desk leaving Lexi to follow her out.

Lexi couldn't imagine her life without the Volt. It wasn't just the obvious stuff; it had saved her from complete isolation when she first arrived. Everywhere else she'd been, she felt rudderless, with no sense of belonging. She'd tried to meet people but failed and ended up disappointed. She outright refused to do the networking events, which were full of people trying to sell her stuff she didn't need. Lexi hated to come across as rude, yet she found no other way to be direct when the planned coffee meeting turned into: "Buy my miracle product, it will change your life."

Other than the runners in her group, she hadn't made friends, yet she had made connections. She got along with the staff and had befriended some of the regular homeless people. What did it say about her that she felt more comfortable doing a jigsaw with a stranger than a lunch date with an over perfumed "consultant" or worse "influencer?"

Anxiety crept over Lexi. The rug was being pulled from her once again. She felt a prickle under her skin and knew that the hives would be visible in a few minutes. Lexi realized she couldn't allow her safe place to be stripped away. Whatever happened next, she couldn't pretend she was doing it only for the community. It was for her sanity.

She would have to do some digging and see what she could come up with. She made no promises, but if there was something she could do to save the Volt, she would. First, she had to finish her actual work; she had to deliver a report and needed to make it a good one; new assignments had been a little thin on the ground recently.

3

Lexi met with Deb and Patrice at Tea and Two most Saturday mornings after their run. It was the perfect place for breakfast and wasn't too fancy that they worried about leaving sweat marks on the chairs. Lexi always had a towel with her just in case and had intimated that on warm days the others should too. Deb gave her the side eye when she made such suggestions. "Is this another rule Lexi? You sure do like them."

They'd met as part of the 5k running group. After the nine-week training program was over and they'd completed the race, they'd agreed to continue training together. Lexi couldn't quite put her finger on what she liked about the group. She could say that they weren't her normal type of friends but she didn't have a type, she'd not had many friends. She was also surprised when organizing plans for running, they didn't complain that she was "bossy" as students at college had, they seemed grateful that she took control.

Patrice was one of those well put together people who seemingly had everything going for her, she rarely appeared flustered, yet there was something going on. Lexi could read people and there was something in Patrice's eyes, like a bird that is constantly on the lookout for predators, she was on edge. Lexi tried to remember if she'd said she previously modeled, she carried herself as if she had, and yet seemed fixated on her weight and her belief that it was a problem.

Deb was the opposite, loud and vivacious, she lived up to the fiery redhead stereotype. She didn't even pretend to be organized, and seemed to be constantly flitting from one place to another, never giving herself enough time. Lexi was scrupulous about timekeeping and hated waiting around for people. She'd almost decided to tell Deb an earlier meetup time than the rest so they didn't have to hang around. Lexi hadn't had time to get to know Amanda, who came for most of the runs but rarely socialized.

Lexi saw that Zander appeared to have a special fondness for them. He hung around and often asked them to test his new specials. She'd learned that his decision to open a cafe with a George Orwell theme hadn't quite worked out. He'd tired of explaining the reason to new customers, and Lexi felt a little sorry for him. Deb like to tease him. "So, tell us again why you thought that a café named after the worst meal in the world was a good idea?"

Thankfully Zander had a good sense of humor. "Actually, I considered Lumpy Blood Pudding, but that was already taken."

Lexi knew he hated to even say the name Tea and Two Slices aloud, mostly referring to it as Tea and Two, which people thought referred to two sugars. She liked the unique idea of naming it after the miserable meal of a cup of tea and two slices of bread and margarine. The author had survived on it in the life he outlined in his novel *Down and Out in Paris and London.*

Lexi tried to cut him a break. "But didn't you say you had some business advice; they must have thought it was a good idea? Though I think it would be better for a bookstore."

Zander rolled his eyes. "They advised me against most of my ideas. You know I was planning to offer an authentic version of tea and two slices as a breakfast item. They didn't think bread and margarine with weak tea would be a big hit."

"I can already see the one-star reviews." Deb joked.

Patrice stopped looking at her phone to interject, her contribution was as unwittingly patronizing as Deb was sarcastic. "But you've got your little author spotlight thingy over there explaining it all." Patrice waved her hand to an Orwell themed display that appeared to have become smaller and less prominent.

As Zander returned to serve a customer, Lexi added, "He is trying to do a good thing here. He gives a ton of stuff away to the Harbor and he buys the best quality food that they grow over at the Eden. I'm hearing some worrying rumors about this place; he might need our support."

Deb was suddenly interested. "Rumors what? Spill I love a good scandal."

Lexi was a little frustrated with Deb. "Everything's not a joke, and don't repeat this but I've heard from someone at the library that there are plans to move them out of here. If that's true, this place could be next."

Patrice was busy adding calories to the app on her phone. "That bagel did not feel like 400 calories."

Deb prodded Patrice to get her attention. "Never mind your calories. Lexi said they might be going to close this place down."

Lexi shushed them both. "I said there is a rumor about the library, that's all. Don't be repeating that. We just need to be supportive."

Patrice put down her phone. "I remember reading the book he based this place on, it was about poverty, misery and hunger, maybe people don't want to think about that stuff over breakfast, it might be time to rethink it."

Lexi hated to admit that Patrice might be right.

Tea and Two was in the main Volt building connected to the library by a brightly lit breezeway, decorated in painted glass by local artists. It was owned by the city. As a business, they leased it at a reduced rate to encourage Volt members to use it. Zander still turned a small profit. Yet there was an unwritten rule that if someone was a little down on their luck, they could eat and pay another time. Those who used the Harbor never took advantage or occupied paying customer's seats. Zander rewarded them with donations of unsold food at the end of each day. Orwell, Lexi mused, would have approved.

Lexi saw Zander looking over, and enjoyed the attention though she would not let him or the group know. She wasn't against the possibility of a relationship, yet had little success in the past. She struggled to talk about this kind of stuff with Lorna, even though her therapist knew everything else about her.

The concern foremost in Lexi's mind was the unfamiliar odors that a man would bring with him. How could she ever bring him, or anyone, back to her apartment? It was the one place she could guarantee was not infected with the detritus of other people's lives. Lorna was teaching her to do some sort of mind chicanery where she could mentally delete smells that bothered her. So far, her experiments in dealing with this part of her obsession showed little promise. Lexi knew humans could not escape their biology, and it wasn't that she didn't have desires; it was all mixed up in her head with her past. Bodies equaled death and decay. She tried to imagine Zander in her apartment, sitting on her sofa. She changed his clothes, gave him a freshly laundered bath robe. That felt better.

He caught her still looking at him, and she groaned inwardly. Did she have a sign over her head saying, "I just dressed you to be more palatable?" Lexi pretended to be engrossed in the conversation that had been going on for the last ten minutes. They were back to their obsession with toilet breaks.

Deb was saying out loud what the others were thinking. She was not shy about sharing her concerns. "What if I need to use the bathroom during the race? I might not be able to hold it."

Patrice looked puzzled. "I believe there are going to be porta-potties."

Deb had already considered this. "If there is a line, it will slow my time down and are you guys going to wait for me?"

Patrice shook her head. "I don't want to run on my own."

Though she had only run the 5K with the training program, Lexi had read everything possible about race habits and etiquette before agreeing to sign up for this longer one. She waited for them to stop talking before giving them a reality check. "Remember, the race is not just a 10K, there's also a half marathon, and lots of faster runners who will have already used the toilets. They will be overflowing and disgusting by the time we get to them. And I hate to burst your bubble, but I don't think a minute or two to stop and pee is going to mess with our race time."

They continued coming up with outlandish and somewhat unhealthy ideas to avoid going to the bathroom. Deb was fretting, "But what if it's not just a pee I need?"

Lexi tried to be encouraging. "It's only an hour or so, you'll be fine, don't eat too late the night before and get up early enough to do what you need to do."

"But I get nervous, and it goes straight to my stomach. Has anyone heard of a *Runner's Flush*? It was on that woman's health site. Patrice let me use your phone to find it. Mine's almost out of battery." Patrice held onto her phone and allowed Deb to search for the article. As they both peered at the screen Lexi looked on with incredulity. Deb beamed victoriously

"Here it is. You do a simple enema before the race. It flushes everything out, so you don't need to go, and you are lighter. You can use it for weight loss too. Look, you can buy a kit."

Lexi dropped her head onto the table in a mock faint and asked. "Do we also add coffee so we don't have…" she was struggling to speak now as the giggles took over. It was the first time she'd laughed like this in as long as she could remember.

Patrice, always looking for another chance to lose a few pounds, continued reading the article.

Zander came over on the pretext of collecting their plates. Lexi was almost doubled up with laughter at this point. "Zander, we have a new menu item for you, it's the Runner's Flush you will need to buy some special tubes though." As she laughed, she accidentally touched his arm. It was only half a second, yet a little spark of magic traveled through her body.

Deb was trying to maintain a position of being annoyed and offended, but eventually she was laughing too. "So, no one wants to come over and administer it for me? Screw you all."

Lexi regained her composure as Zander went back to cleaning tables. It was time to be serious. "Please remember we only have two more midweek runs before the race, I don't want to have to track you down. No excuses, okay? And what are we going to do about this Nathan guy? He seems to have attached himself to us, which is okay on our training runs, but what happens in the race? He's a bit of a loose cannon."

Patrice looked up from her phone and smiled. "Oh he's harmless, even if he has some funny ideas."

Lexi sighed. "I know we aren't an official group, but we have been running together for months. Nathan tagging along more regularly makes it look like he's part of us. Some of his funny ideas could get us kicked out of the race. He has a gripe against the city and is planning to run the race without registering as a protest. Some call it running "bandit"–running the race route alongside the other runners, but not paying the registration fee. Nathan has some notion about the race fees not being used correctly."

"He might be right, it's expensive and last time they didn't even have enough water," Deb said seriously.

"That may be the case," Lexi said, "but there's a time and a place for protest. I find it safer to follow the rules."

"If he runs the race without registering there's nothing we can do, unless you plan to outrun him. You're overthinking this Lexi. Nathan isn't our problem." Deb took the last bite of her breakfast bagel brushing off the crumbs that had accumulated on her chest. "As long as he doesn't think he's getting any of my pre-race donuts, he can do what he likes."

It impressed Lexi that Deb had identified her kryptonite—overthinking was exactly right.

Lexi was the last to leave. She took a moment to consider the disaster zone that was the area where Deb had been sitting, how could she have made such a mess? Lexi in contrast had left no trace that she had ever been there. Zander came over to clean up, seemingly unfazed by the pile of torn up sugar packets and crumbs. Though Lexi needed to leave, she had left it too late as Zander began to engage her in conversation. "I know you've been coming here for a while but I can't remember if you ever told me, are you from here? I can never figure your accent."

Lexi had to think how to answer without revealing too much. It was hard to explain that she'd lived close to Tribune but could have been anywhere, it was as if she'd lived in a vacuum. There was no one accent at The Sanctuary, it was like an international community. "Not too far away and I've travelled a little." She changed the subject, "I hope Deb doesn't bother you too much, she doesn't mean any harm."

"I know she likes to joke but does everyone think this place is a joke, all the Orwell stuff?"

"You are trying to make a difference. Maybe there's a better way to do it, though. I'm not an expert, but you need to find a way to tell the cafe's story in a more enticing way."

Zander became animated. "I have some other ideas. Would you be willing to meet and talk them over sometime? I'm sure you would be a great help."

Lexi saw the opportunity, but at the last minute, her overthinking grabbed the reins. Her flutter of excitement was quickly replaced with an avalanche of thoughts about everything that could go wrong. "You know Patrice might be more help. I heard her say she has a background in interior design and I'm sure it included marketing."

Lexi saw that Zander looked crestfallen. She left the building to spend another weekend alone.

4

———

Lexi had to go downtown. Though she could do most of her work remotely. Today she had to go to the office of Underosa Communications, a Public Relations company, and her biggest client. Lexi had worked for them on an independent contractor basis for eighteen months. They paid so well she had stopped chasing other clients and it had become her main stream of income.

Lexi liked the assignments, yet the in-person meetings made her uncomfortable. She never worried about the quality of her work. The company recognized she was excellent at her job and had learned to leave her alone as long as she "executed efficiently and on time." The meetings sometimes meant a change of direction in her work. She worried they would push her to do something unethical. Even though she'd been clear which lines she wouldn't cross, and she would never compromise her values. She knew PR meant bending the truth a little, the equivalent of white lies.

Today the meeting room felt different. Lexi realized the energy had changed because a woman she wasn't expecting was sat at the table.

"I'm not sure we've met, I'm Celeste Collins. Underosa Communications has been hired to undertake a project that may become controversial, and it therefore requires complete confidentiality. They have asked me, their legal counsel, to take the lead on this project. Though we've never asked you to do this in the past, this contract will require you to sign a Non-Disclosure Agreement."

The presence of a lawyer in place of the people she usually worked with was a surprise, and more so, that it was Celeste Collins. Lexi knew of her in her capacity as leader of the Tutus running group. A fund-raising group of ladies who lunched, and ran races in fancy tutus and full makeup and jewelry. Lexi reminded herself that was not the group's actual name but what Deb had dubbed them. She'd better not use it by accident. Celeste's business attire was straight out of a glossy TV show, she had rarely seen anyone so exquisitely put together in real life. Though Lexi preferred her own simple style, she couldn't help but admire Celeste's choice of silk and cashmere. She looked dressed for something bigger than a local deal.

Celeste continued, "Once you've signed, we'll give you your brief. If you decide you can't complete it as required, we won't need you for further assignments. On the plus side, the work comes with a considerable bonus payment on completion of your report."

So, she had no choice. Sign and find out too late if it was a raw deal. If she refused to go ahead, they would fire her. Lexi had a sickly feeling in her stomach. She tried to focus on the positive. She had some money saved, though it wasn't enough to live on forever. It wouldn't last long without regular income. The company had never asked her to do anything too sketchy, although she wondered if her moral compass was off and whether what she was prepared to do these days would have horrified her former self. Though she wasn't sure if she could walk away without knowing what she was turning down.

Celeste saw she had reservations. "Why not take a break. Get some fresh air and have a little time to think about it."

"Okay, I'll get some lunch and be back in a couple of hours."

Celeste had already moved on and was looking at some papers on her desk. "Take your time."

Lexi felt she had been dismissed like a naughty schoolgirl. As she stepped out of the building into the now cooling fall sunshine, she felt relieved to be out of Underosa and wished that she didn't have to return. Whatever the job was, it wasn't good. What controversial stuff were they involved with in the town? She had never seen Underosa work with a lawyer. Most of the work was small time. Though when they began offering her contracts for Reputation Management, it was on behalf of bigger clients from outside of the area. Maybe this was the company's way of becoming a bigger fish.

She headed to the downtown coffee bar, where she knew there would be a pile of local newspapers. Time to go old school and see what the locals were talking about in the letters to the editor pages. She found a booth and ordered a caramel something-or-other dessert parading as coffee. A luxury she soon might not be able to afford.

People were idiots, Lexi thought while reading the local paper—The Trib. They voted against their interests and ranted about things that were none of their business. One letter caught her eye: it was from another of the running group, Amanda, in her official capacity: Dr. Amanda Lucas—local environmentalist and sometimes-broadcaster. She'd written to explain to the public that they needed to care about what was under their feet and how the litter they dropped was damaging to wildlife. She was rallying against those who refused a straw in a restaurant to save the environment, and then bought fast food and dropped their trash that ended up in the bayou. Lexi wondered how Amanda could stand it. Her phone-in show was overwhelmingly littered—no pun intended—with people asking ridiculous questions. Amanda also oversaw the Eden, the Volt's Community Garden. They ran classes that taught residents to grow their own food, and supplied Tea and Two with fresh vegetables.

The train of thought distracted Lexi. She was unlikely to find what she needed here. She was playing for time, running down the clock even though that wouldn't achieve anything.

Lost in this thought for a moment, she heard a familiar voice.

"Cheating on Tea and Two on a school day?"

She looked up to see Zander; at the same moment, a small headline caught her eye. A motion to change the use of a building. She looked back to the newspaper. It would have been easy for him to think that she was ignoring him. After a pause, she looked up. "Hi sorry, I'm working on something, please give me a minute."

"I'm going to get a coffee. Want anything?"

Lexi shook her head and trained her focus back to her dilemma, she wanted someone to tell her what to do, not the soft and reassuring voice of Lorna telling her, "But Lexi, you know the answer it is within you, you just have to listen." Maybe Lorna was right, or maybe, she wondered, had the universe dropped Zander here right now to help her? He returned with an espresso.

Lexi pointed to his tiny cup. "Not planning on staying long?"

"I have a meeting with the bank manager. I don't want to be running to the bathroom as he shares the bad news. Unless you've got one of your friend's weird running solutions involving tubes?"

Lexi laughed. "Smart business owner like you. I'm sure they'll be begging to give you more money."

"Ha, I wish. I really don't want to think about it right now. Let's talk about something else."

They chatted about the Volt. It was the only thing they had in common. They'd never met outside of that building. She realized though she liked him; she knew little about him. "Did you ride here on a skateboard?" She was trying to lighten the mood. His messy hair and skater style made him appear younger. Though he had made a bit of an effort for his meeting, he seemed like he had more on his mind than which shirt he had put on that morning. She was glad to have someone to talk to, and wondered about sharing her own dilemma. "Can I ask for your advice?" She didn't wait for his answer. "I can't give you all the details as I don't know them myself, but I might be about to walk into some trouble. The company I work with has offered me a confidential assignment. My job sometimes requires me to write reports that justify one side of an argument usually on behalf of a company or organization. I think it might be something to do with this, but I can't know for sure." Lexi pointed to what she'd been reading when he'd arrived.

There was a lot of legal jargon in the notice that Zander didn't seem to get. "Explain it to me like I'm five."

"It appears to give the City the right to sell off—or change the use of—any building it currently owns. It also allows them to change previously signed agreements under an 'Emergency Budget Mandate.'"

"I still don't see where you come into it."

Lexi was wondering how much to share. It was all still theory, though she was almost certain she was correct in her suspicions. She sat back in her chair, took a deep breath, and lowered her voice. "Imagine a beautiful building that serves the community. Everyone loves it whether they go to drink coffee, borrow a book, or practice yoga. It sits overlooking a relaxing waterfront. On the other side of that water are million-dollar homes. Now imagine there are a group of people who don't think that land should be wasted on the losers and drug abusers—not my words! If they could make it easier for them to sell it to the highest bidder, do you think they would?"

Zander audibly gulped as he understood the implications of the tiny piece in the paper. He took a moment to process what she was telling him. "So, if you're right, what if you take the assignment and see what you can do to make it work for the other party? If you are wrong, you've nothing to lose either way."

"How? If they want me to dish some dirt, I'm not sure how that could work for the other party as you call it?"

He leaned over and looked directly into her eyes while casually touching her arm. "Who else would you trust to do this job and make sure that they do it fairly, no matter what the issue is? Do you think the next person in line is going to be as worried about the ethics of it? And there's no guarantee that you'll find what they want you to. You might discover something else."

He was right. They would hire someone else, and she would have missed the opportunity. She still felt that she was excusing her own future poor choices but felt a little clearer. Unfortunately, if she was right, this decision would affect him, too.

Zander had an idea. "You know who might help? Amanda, the radio show presenter who runs the Eden. You know her right? I've seen you in the Volt with her."

Lexi looked unsure. "She runs with us sometimes, though she doesn't hang around to chat. Why do you think she could help?"

Zander smiled. "Just trust me on this one, she's got her ear to the ground and cares about the community. She would fight to protect the Volt."

While they were chatting, they overheard a loud conversation from the next booth. The woman was regaling her lunch partner with stories of her running. "When I ran the marathon," and "well as a marathon runner," and even, "when you are a marathon runner you can eat whatever you want."

Lexi and Zander locked eyes, stifling giggles. It was clear the silent recipient of the bragging woman couldn't get a word in, and the woman went on and on. She did it for charity, of course. They raised *thousands* for... the voice trailed off as food arrived at the table.

As Zander and Lexi stood up to leave, she turned her head to get a good look at the woman. She had half guessed that she was one of the Tutus. Lexi had never been a fan of the group who mainly liked to be seen handing over checks and doing fun runs while sipping martinis, she liked them even less now she was having to deal with Celeste. She almost made a snarky comment but held her tongue. She realized as they headed out into the street that she cared what Zander thought about her.

As Lexi walked back towards the Underosa Communications building, she was still torn. She took a turn around the block, weighing her decision. She could walk away, let someone else worry about it. But what if she was right and the report was to support the demise of the Volt. Yet, she reasoned with herself, her job was putting together the facts, the client was responsible for framing the argument. It wouldn't be the first time a client was disappointed when they found that the evidence they wanted to support their cause didn't exist, no matter which way they twisted what they had. Maybe this was an opportunity, a chance to do something that mattered.

She made her decision on the second walk around the block, but went around a third time. She didn't want to curse her decision. Thankfully, no one noticed she always did things in threes, even Lorna didn't know that she still held onto this ritual. Lexi entered the office, on a mission to do all she could to make sure they couldn't sacrifice the Volt. She would be a double agent. Whatever they wanted her to do, she would smile, agree, and sign. What she did after that was not for them to know.

Lexi listened while Celeste gave her the sales pitch for the assignment. The lawyer probably knew that what she was leading up to might meet with resistance. Lexi looked at Celeste, who fake smiled back at her as she presented the NDA, a detailed and scary document full of confusing legal jargon. Lexi wouldn't be allowed to talk about her work for a year after she'd completed it, whatever the outcome. They could use her findings in whatever form they wanted. Some of the information was already publicly available. She needed to prove she had acted in good faith and done all she could to abide by the agreement. The only positive was that they were paying her a golden "keep your mouth shut" bonus.

After Lexi signed, Celeste outlined the assignment. She talked of "austerity measures, maximization of public funding, relocation of resources." Then she said what Lexi had dreaded hearing. "The city has many beautiful areas. People are keen to come here. We shouldn't keep it all to ourselves. We can put libraries, homeless shelters, and business centers anywhere. But to take up the best place on the water for people to hang round there instead of getting a job, that's such a waste." As Lexi had guessed, they wanted to close the Volt or break it up and move it. If she hadn't met Zander, she might have taken the easier route and walked away.

Celeste continued, "There are many more suitable places for a resource such as the Volt, and having it centralized makes people a little well—lazy." Celeste's voice had morphed into a high-pitched southern drawl. Lexi recognized the shift from Celeste's baseline behavior. In the little time she'd observed her it was enough to see a hint of desperation. She was lying about something. She guessed Celeste wasn't just the lawyer; she was part of whatever was going on.

"What is it that the city hopes to do with the land or property?"

Celeste had the brief ready to give to Lexi. "As you have now signed the agreement, I can give you the information you need to get started on your report. Who or what might come next is on a need-to-know basis. As of right now, you don't need that information."

Lexi wondered what the client could have offered to induce Underosa to take this project on. Maybe they were being blackmailed into it. During her previous assignment briefings, they still seemed to have some values.

"We're sure you can come up with evidence that the low-income families who use the facilities would be comfortable in a more suitable neighborhood, and not in such an imposing building. The homeless will also be better served in a location closer to the hostels that are there for that very reason, or even close to the highway so they can move on. We expect you to find a list of suitable neighborhoods that can fulfill both their needs. You have all the financial data you need to persuade any detractors that the Volt is a money pit that serves only a minority of the town."

So, it was not just the building they wanted; it was the people they didn't. They were looking for evidence to support the gentrification of the waterfront area with no thought of the people the Volt served or the people who worked there. Lexi's smile was getting harder to fake. She was burning with anger and had to force herself to stay focused so she wouldn't betray her disgust.

Celeste concluded speaking and told her she had just over a month to prepare a report. They planned to announce their findings at a town council meeting.

Lexi didn't know how she was going to make this work; how could she discover and use the data to support the Volt instead of destroying it? Zander had once told her that Tea and Two was on a relatively inexpensive short-term lease. He believed it worked in his business's favor. If things took a downturn, it didn't tie him into an expensive commitment. The change in rules would mean they could throw him out without warning. If that happened, he would struggle to find somewhere else he could afford.

Where could she even start? One month barely gave her time to do her research, never mind her dual plan of proving the opposite of their argument. She was going to have to do some fast, deep digging to get to the bottom of this.

5

Lᴇxɪ ꜰᴏʟʟᴏᴡᴇᴅ Zander's advice to talk to Amanda, who agreed to meet her at the Eden. Lexi arrived early enough to get coffee, and hoped to catch Zander though he was nowhere around. She took a self-service coffee available for payment via an honesty box, and walked through the Atrium. Adding a few pieces to the community jigsaw would help to clear her head.

Joshua was sitting looking at the picture on the box of a brand-new puzzle. She'd only recently learned his name. He was often the only person in this quiet area of the Volt. Though she normally preferred to be alone, she found his presence unobtrusive. He seemed to know when to speak and when to give her peace. Today she wanted to talk. "Too scared to even start this one?"

"Sometimes it's good to have a plan before jumping in."

How did he always know the right thing to say? They sat in silence for a while and then he began assembling the border while she sipped her coffee. Lexi thought of all the projects she'd completed. She'd never needed anyone else. She'd convinced herself she could manage her life on her own. Lorna had for years pushed her to let down her guard and make connections. Now, for the first time, she realized she needed allies—people she could trust. She needed help to find some wiggle room in the deal she'd made with the devil.

Lexi had seen enough to know that Amanda was an outlier in the town, she seemed to have some influence and respect, but Lexi was almost certain, she wouldn't be supportive of any plan that would jeopardize the future of the Volt especially as she was part of it. Yet she wasn't sure how much she should share or what Amanda could do to help.

In movies people gathered for secret meetings in Churches, the gangsters made their plans; the police met their informants. Meeting in a community garden seemed like a suitable alternative. Lexi arrived early and saw that Amanda was in the Eden's tiny office. She was sitting with her back to Lexi and was engaged in an animated and evidently heated telephone call.

Lexi glanced at a display about sea turtles. She approached the office when Amanda hung up, but was rudely heckled. A parrot flew onto a perch above her head. "Intruder, stop, turn around, I'll shoot your ass, don't try me."

"You've met Jasper I see." The parrot flew to Amanda's shoulder. It looked like it could probably take an eye out, though it seemed happy enough with Amanda. "Jasper is an African Grey parrot; he's probably been alive for around thirty years and could live to up to sixty and he's way smarter than most of the idiots who call into my radio show."

Lexi sympathized with Amanda's frustration about dealing with idiots.

"Parrots are highly intelligent beings, yet it seems we've relegated their role to learning curse words that are the primary vocabulary of many parrot 'owners'." As she used air quotes to emphasize the word owner, the parrot on cue demonstrated her point. "Fuck off, Fuck you, Fuckety Fuckface."

Amanda rolled her eyes and continued. "When people get

bored with the latest genetically modified breed of dog, or the snake has disappeared down the back of the sofa, the showoff pet-owner turns their attention to parrots, macaws, lamas even. We recently had to rescue an emu from a duplex, or rather rescue its human. Birds need to be out in the wild. They end up here in this simulated habitat, it's the best we can do. Jasper was part of the family until he ran out of swear words and became entangled in mom's knitting. So, what can I do for you, found a cat that thinks it's a tiger?"

The outburst had caught her by surprise. "I'm familiar with the Ask Amanda show. I don't know how you tolerate most of the callers."

Amanda softened. "I'm so sorry for ranting. You must wonder what you've walked into. I just had some bad news. Please tell me what I can do to help, or what you would like to know?"

"Why don't you take a moment, maybe show me around? Or is there anything I can help you with? I'm a good listener."

Amanda sat back in her chair and sighed. "Every day this place stays open is the result of a battle. We survive on a shoestring budget. Whereas the other areas of the Volt have some City money, we're mostly funded by a charity—and they just told me they will not renew the grant. I already do a lot of work for free. I need another funding body, but the process will take months. I expected this grant to be renewed in the new year."

"Were you given any warning, any suggestion of why now?"

Amanda pondered. "This all just happened, so I need to figure out if there's anything else going on, but they said something curious. If I consider moving the Eden to a different part of town, they might find money from their Low-Income Neighborhood Fund."

"I knew it!" Lexi was sure she had come to the right person.

Amanda looked puzzled. "You knew what?"

"I was unsure if I dared share my suspicions about something that's happening locally. My work means I'm bound by an NDA though I'd already discovered some information before I signed it. If I can guide you to what's publicly available and you can assure me no-one will think it came from me, we might be of help to each other."

"Lexi, you can trust me. Tell me what you know and what it might have to do with my funding problems. I really should be on the phone trying to figure out my next move. If I don't, Jasper here is going to be homeless, along with the rest of the rescue animals."

With a resigned look, Lexi said. "There are rumors that the Volt is in danger of being sold off and services relocated. I've already heard that there are plans to move the library. It looks like your charity might be colluding with whoever is behind the plan to make it happen."

Amanda paused before saying. "The town planners here are short sighted. I've suspected something big was coming that would hurt the local environment and the town. Tell me what you can and point me to where I can find out more."

They talked for over an hour, then they drew a map and noted everyone they suspected might have a stake in the plans. The charity that had been funding the Eden had previous links with some of the big property developers in town, and Celeste Collins often featured in their fundraisers. The degrees of separation in Tribune were a lot closer than six.

Amanda saw a spark of an idea. "I don't have a solution for what's going on in the town but I'd like a meeting with our running group. I have an idea that could be fun and might give us a reason to be seen with each other so we can share information. When are we next getting together?"

6

LEXI DIDN'T KNOW what Amanda had planned; she'd just made the arrangements for the running group to meet. The group was intrigued and a little excited about the meeting. Though they often met at Tea after midweek runs, Lexi asked that they all be here.

"So, I wonder what she wants?" Deb directed the question at Lexi. "I mean, she must want something, right? She's not been exactly sociable since she started running with us. Y'all know what I'm talking about." Deb became more southern as she became excited. "Isn't she some sort of professor? I'm always scared of saying something dumb." Amanda arrived before they could say any more and looked quizzically at the group, who all appeared guilty of something. She was a striking figure in her camel coat and hand-painted knee-length boots, in contrast to the group in their running gear. "So, what did I miss?"

Nathan opened his mouth, about to make mischief.

Lexi jumped in, "We are all curious about how we can help you."

Patrice, who until now, had been purely observing, asked. "Those boots, are they Pitzellas?"

Amanda was impressed. "How?"

"I used to be in design, I worked on his house."

"You must be good. Everything he does is spectacular."

Patrice's face betrayed a mixture of emotions, pride, and sadness among them. "It was one of the last jobs I did before I closed my business."

Zander appeared and refilled their drinks. When he returned, Amanda pointed to an empty chair. "Come and join us." Amanda began by giving them some background to her work and the radio show she needed help with. "I guess you know I host the Ask Amanda show. It's only a small part of my work. I spend most of my time on research related to the environment. The station would like to make the show more regular and prominent, and pay me directly. The charity that I currently work for only loans me to them, and they may not be hiring me for much longer. Between these walls I will tell you, I never wanted to do Ask Amanda in the first place, however as part of my role, they required me to educate the public in an entertaining and accessible way. It offers free advertising for the charity. Unfortunately, in my attempts to focus on the educational element, the show has been losing ratings and until recently the station discussed taking it off the air. That was, until we started getting some of the more unusual questions."

Nathan perked up. "Ah, you mean the mysterious Trib Trib Tiger, or was it a panther?"

Deb looked annoyed. "Why is he here, anyway? Are you part of our group now?"

Amanda smiled "I invited him. Nathan is a friend, and you might need him if you accept the mission I'm about to propose."

"Well then, can we get to the point? I need to feed my cats."

Lexi had noticed Deb was becoming territorial about the group, and suspected she didn't have many friends. It seemed something everyone sitting around the table had in common.

"If you subscribe to the notion that there is no such thing as a stupid question, the show will prove you wrong. The station encourages the stupid questions. People like to feel they are smarter than those who call in. So, when someone asks if their dead cat has gone to heaven or how come the fountain is frozen if global warming is real? People lap it up."

Patrice looked up from her phone where she'd been answering a text. "So, you need us to call in and act like dumbasses."

The group erupted in laughter, and Amanda tried to pull it back together.

"I need a balance of callers. Some new people to keep the show alive. I have a few good callers who I can rely on to help the show keep a little dignity, but they are not what the studio is interested in. They want less science, and more sass. We're competing with shows whose listeners have a daily diet of conspiracy theories, half-truths and local scandal. I need reliable callers who are on the right side of crazy, and that's where you come in. Some of you have proved you already have exactly what I'm looking for."

Deb blushed. Her face matched the titian hue of her hair—though she liked to call it strawberry blonde.

"So, Deb, do tell us, was it a moonlit night when you saw the tiger chasing your cat through the back streets of Tribune?"

Deb looked to the rest of the group for support and eventually raised her hands in surrender. "Okay, yes, one of those calls was me. I had a rough meeting and came home and had a few drinks. I heard your show, and you were asking people to call in. I thought I was doing you a favor. It was more plausible than the guy before me. You cut him off for saying lizard people ran the town. How did you know it was me?"

Lexi had been following the conversation with amusement.

"Deb you can tell your voice a mile off, especially when you've had a drink."

Deb looked at Lexi, "When have you seen me drunk? Oh, hang on, I guess you were at the after-race party."

Amanda reminded her, "You also gave your real name part way through the call after you'd originally given a false one."

Deb became excited. "So, how will it work? What do you want us to do? I can do different voices."

Amanda explained she needed genuine people, but just as reality shows are somewhat scripted, she would give them some pointers on what to look for. "I need more than just callers. I need a street team. While you are out running, you will record or report what you see and where possible call in to the show live with questions and sightings. Occasionally I might ask you to look out for species, information that I can use in research."

Zander, who had been listening quietly, raised his hand. "I'm confused. Was there ever a tiger and why am I here?"

Amanda smiled. "As far as we know, there isn't a tiger, though since the original call from Deb, we have had many other callers that believe they have seen something. Unless it has escaped from a zoo or been reared illegally, or some rare species that's found its way up here. It's probably just an overfed house cat.

Deb spoke up again; "Hey, I might have been drunk, but I wasn't making it up I saw something,"

Amanda seemed surprised. "Deb, maybe you've never heard of the boy who cried wolf? How many other crank calls were from you? Were you also responsible for the scare about radioactive glow-in-the-dark carrots?"

Lexi wanted to tie things up. "I have questions. What's in it for us? And if we want to do it, how will it work? You run at the same time as us, and sometimes the show is on when it is dark."

"Yes, the schedule moves around, and sometimes it sounds

live but is pre-recorded, though I want some live call-ins to encourage others to do it. And what's in it for you? I can't pay you, but I can get you freebies from the station concert/sports tickets etc. and you might help save the planet—and my job. Oh, and Zander to your other question, we want you to host trainings and educational tie-ins, and for that we are looking for ways to pay."

"I'm in, if I don't have to do the calls." Lexi said.

Deb asked, "I can't wait. Do we have a name?"

"Actually, you do. Collectively you'll be the Prowling Panthera's."

As Deb groaned, Amanda said, "Be grateful, I'm getting in first before the station come up with a tacky name like the Foxy Ladies."

Deb asked, "Can we have our own Glass Jelly fan page? We can have our photos taken and people can send us tips to look out for."

Before Amanda could answer Lexi jumped in. "I don't do social media so if you go down that route you can count me out. Glass Jelly is the worst. They just divide everyone into tribes."

Amanda reassured Lexi. "We are focused on the wildlife, the radio station has its own Glass Jelly page and a website, we will only post pictures of animals not people."

Deb tossed her hair back in a mock flounce. "Well, maybe I'll make my own page. It might get me some business once people know I'm a Panthera."

Amanda chose to ignore Deb's reply. "You can start next week. Keep your eyes open for anything interesting during the race. Sorry I can't be with you this time, but I'll be cheering you on. I'm sure you'll have more fun than I will judging the kid's animal-themed race."

Everyone agreed to be part of the fun. Lexi stayed behind to talk to Amanda. "So, what's going on, do you have a new job with the station?"

Amanda shook her head. "Not exactly, they've always said they'd pay me independently if they could have more control on the content. I've put in a proposal for a more expanded show, they've agreed in principle. You guys are my unique selling point."

"And the charity, have you given them an answer regarding a potential move?"

"They don't know I'm aware of the bigger Volt picture. I'm letting them think I'm looking for other funders for the Eden. Maybe I can push them into telling me there won't be an Eden. I've got a little time before the funding runs out."

"I'm happy to help. So let me know if there's anything I can do. Though I am a little confused, how is this going to help save the Volt?"

Amanda smiled. "I'm not going to pretend I have a plan just yet, but it will be harder for them to close the Volt if its profile is raised positively within the community, and I might have some more tricks up my sleeve. It would be worth you coming over to the studio sometime. Get a feel for how the show works and my ideas for reviving it. No disrespect to the others Lexi, but I trust you, along with Nathan we could make an excellent team to look at ideas to save the Volt. I think we should meet up again."

"I'd like that," she said. "Meanwhile I'll look out for you at the race."

Lexi liked Amanda's no-nonsense approach. There was something reassuringly confident about her, and she wondered if she dared to hope for more. Maybe they could become friends.

7

THIS WAS the first time Deb had woken up and not known where she was. It was like one of those movies where the drunken hero wakes up and turns to discover a stranger lying next to them. Yet she was alone. Deb had, according to her friends, become wild and reckless since she became widowed after losing her husband to an aggressive form of cancer. The truth was a little less dramatic. She was still only thirty-five, she'd spent two years grieving, she just wanted some fun. She was much more careful than she let on. She took calculated risks, or that is what she told herself, and she hadn't gone out with any plans to stay out all night. She didn't fit in with the old crowd from when she was married, as much as they tried to include her. She was tired of being the only single one at every gathering. She was ready for her life to restart.

Deb was still pondering how she'd got there, when a man she struggled to recognize—looking like one of those ripped guys with abs on a romance novel cover—came out of what she guessed was the bathroom. Now it was coming back to her. She wouldn't have come back here with just anyone. Maybe this hadn't been such a mistake after all. Before she had time to luxuriate in a fantasy relationship, the man picked up her balled-up clothes and tossed them onto the bed.

"Time to get up and out of here. My wife gets off night shift in an hour."

As the memories of the night before started to come back to her, she realized what today was; it was Race Day. She didn't even know where the start line was from here, wherever here was. This was not a good start. Maybe her friends had been right. She had been reckless. Deb had to get out of there and get ready for the race. The guy's voice was drifting in and out of her brain, talking about warm water and towels, telling her to clean herself up. "I'm not sure where we are," she admitted. "I need to get back home."

"You can find a cab on the corner. Sorry we have to leave it like this, but I explained last night that you would have to be gone early."

The cab ride was embarrassing. The drive of shame was worse than the walk of the same name. If she could remember, she might have been proud that she'd lived a little. She had no recollection of the journey to the location she was leaving. Shit, shit, shit, she was going to have to think of an excuse why she wouldn't be at the meetup location, if she could make it at all. She would have to call Lexi.

They didn't have the type of relationship where you had actual phone conversations. Did anyone anymore? They arranged their meetings by text or social media. She didn't think she'd ever spoken to Lexi on the phone. Deb knew she had a reputation for being flaky, and it wouldn't surprise them if she let them down. She had no intention of doing so. She would feed the cats and then she had to make the call.

8

———

Lexi was awake before the alarm. She had set three, just in case. Even though she'd slept reasonably well, race day had her jittery. Why couldn't the rest of them take it seriously? Though they showed up for the training runs, they were constantly thinking up excuses for skipping them. The seemed to think that her detailed schedules and training plan was unnecessary. They had been training for months, but still seemed to think it was some kind of joke. Yes they ran, but they didn't seem to care if they got any faster. Lexi needed a team that supported her, yet she knew that she also needed them in her life. They kept her balanced, stopped her from spiraling out of control.

Looking around in the early morning light at her pristine apartment, she was aware of how different she was to the rest of her new group of friends. They were sometimes chaotic and silly, traits that she struggled to relate to. There was nothing unnecessary, frivolous, or fluffy in her surroundings. It was vital that she could easily lay her hands on the items she needed to function optimally. She'd laid her running clothes out in the order she would need them, with a spare set just in case, she wasn't sure what the "case" might be. Oh yes, she remembered;

the story of someone forgetting their running shoes and only discovering it the night before the race. It had sent shivers down her spine.

Lexi refused to acknowledge any of her concerns as a problem. Anxiety was worrying about things that might not happen. Lexi worried about scenarios that not only could happen, they had happened, there were documented cases. She wanted to check the mail, though until it was time to leave, she never went outside of the apartment on the day of an important event. Getting locked out and being in the cold trying to remember a phone number was high on her list of private terrors. Who would she call in an emergency anyway? Deb said she needed to lighten up, allow some messiness in her life. Where was the fun if you controlled everything?

Today she had a race to run and however the others wanted to play it, she was out to at least beat her personal record from her trainings. She didn't plan to waste time stopping to chat. The group liked to take it easy on training runs. It was more like a social hour. They could probably think of a thousand reasons not to run. Today there would be no excuses and although they had agreed to support each other and try to stay at the same pace, Lexi wasn't making any promises. If she found her second wind, she was going with it.

She wondered how Patrice would do. This would be her first race after the 5k and although she joined in the camaraderie and fun, she seemed often to have stuff on her mind. Lexi wondered if there was pressure from her husband. They'd never met him, though Patrice was always rushing off to some dinner or event that he had made it clear he expected her to attend. Maybe he would show up later. Lexi kind of hoped not. He sounded a bit of a dick.

And then there was Nathan. He tagged along and, to be fair, his opinionated discussions were sometimes a welcome relief from the fluffy stuff that was normally on offer, though sometimes she didn't want to think about heavy stuff either, not after writing about it all day. She wanted to switch off and run and win. She couldn't believe that they'd chosen this race because they liked the medal. Really. A medal. They were cool looking, yet Lexi would've preferred to have done a race in a neighboring town where she could be certain she was anonymous. If she placed in the race she might end up with her face in the local paper. No one had recognized her for years, yet it still worried her. She went along with the plan because she valued the group. They didn't seem to judge her; they didn't know her, weren't aware of her past. They didn't even know her real name.

Lexi heard a phone ringing, she didn't recognize her own ringtone. She never answered her phone—never. Occasionally, someone would find an article and track her down, wanting to do an interview. She not only refused, but she also lied, told them the person they were looking for had deceased long ago. She knew they could easily find out it wasn't true; she didn't care; it made them work a little harder. If they tried again they would find their number blocked. The noise kept on until she finally looked at the phone and recognized Deb's number. So, she was going to bail on them? Figures. She had been behaving strangely the last few runs and seemed jumpy.

While she tied her shoes, Lexi played the message. It was not what she expected. Deb was rambling. She didn't sound like her usual easy-going self.

"Lexi, I think this is your number, but, Oh, just please call me back. I want to do the race honestly, but something... look, just call me back or come to my place. I'll text the address."

In her messages was indeed Deb's address. Lexi replied, confirming she was heading to the apartment. She'd planned to do a walk to warm up for the race and decided this ten-minute journey would suffice. Lexi wondered how Deb managed financially. She always seemed to have enough, but she didn't appear to do a lot of work. Consultant was her description, which seem to cover a multitude of odd jobs and weird assignments.

The look of relief when Deb answered the door was profound. "Thanks for coming. I'm sorry, I've got myself into a bit of a mess."

Lexi looked at her running watch. "Okay, you said you want to run the race. If that's true you need to tell me what's going on, we don't have a lot of time."

"I've just woken up in the apartment of a married man who I slept with last night. I don't remember how I got there, and his wife was on her way home. And I don't do married men, by the way."

Lexi listened while she helped Deb search for her running shoes. There was no surface that was clean. She helped to pin her crumpled race bib to her shirt. Whatever else had happened the night before, she had kept hold of her race packet. The state of Deb's apartment would drive Lexi back into full-time therapy. There was at least six months' worth of cat hair clinging to Deb's running clothes.

"I was running late. I went to see a client who wanted a last-minute meeting. I only just made it to the hotel to collect my packet. There was a comedy show in the hotel bar, so I got some bar food and a drink. I only planned to have one. I took something."

"A drug you mean?"

"I was talking to a guy at the bar. He asked if I had cats because I had cat hair on my jacket. He offered me a pill, said it was cat valium and it would make me feel good. I don't believe he told me he was married, but this morning he claimed he had."

"Cat Valium, you know that's a street name for ketamine? It's not only illegal, but it can also be dangerous."

Deb looked at Lexi as if she was seeing a different side to her. "I didn't, but I'm surprised you do."

So much about the situation made Lexi uncomfortable yet her feelings came from concern for Deb rather than judgement. It could have been so much worse.

"Are you sure you feel up to running? There might be other side effects, that concern about digestive issues could become a reality. There's no shame in skipping this one."

Deb looked like she was still thinking over what had happened "There's no way he told me he was married. He was lying."

"Deb, even if you think you went with this guy willingly, it certainly seems that he took advantage, he gave you a powerful drug and took you back to his apartment. And who was he, have you ever seen him before?"

Deb looked embarrassed. "I don't think so, and I vaguely remember him asking if I was prepared to get freaky. I can't blame him. I was flattered. He was young, younger than me anyway, maybe in his twenties. All I wanted was a drink to forget a mess I'd got myself into, and I went and walked into another one. Let's just go run."

Lexi wondered what other mess Deb was in but thought better of asking. She couldn't imagine putting herself in a vulnerable position like Deb had. Lexi had never, would never, allow herself to be out of control like that.

Deb found her running shoes, and they headed out to the start line in silence.

9

Patrice wasn't sure how, but her left arm no longer worked. It was still attached to her body, yet she couldn't move it with her thoughts or her actions. She lifted it with her other hand, and it dropped lifelessly. It felt like it weighed at least fifty pounds. How much did each of the parts of her body weigh, she wondered? And could she run a race without her left arm? As she pondered this, the life came back into it, pins and needles danced throughout the lifeless limb, and she squirmed with discomfort. She'd slept on the sofa—again.

Her first big race and she had to sacrifice sleep and comfort because Frank was being an asshole. He hadn't always been like this. He was a good man who cared about her, and had encouraged her with running. It had been helpful in finally feeling settled in this new town. She'd ordered new running gear. Unfortunately, they had arrived only yesterday. She was unsure if it was a good idea to wear something new on a day already fraught with anxiety. She tried them on, and Frank was passing her dressing room as she was admiring herself in the mirror.

"Turn around and let me see my little running wife."

She turned to face him, expecting him to like what he saw. The training had helped to tighten up her saggy bits, and she was pleased with the definition that was developing in her muscles. Instead, he looked with horror, then apparent humor that became a flicker of anger.

"You can't wear the leggings, surely you can see that?" He almost spat the words at her.

"What do you mean? I like them, they fit well. They are comfortable and I like the pocket for my phone."

He rolled his eyes and shook his head. She looked in the mirror, auditing her body, trying to figure out what he was seeing. Her rear end had never been so defined. Maybe the leggings were a little tight, but running gear was supposed to be snug, wasn't it? She was losing confidence in what she'd believed only minutes ago. Frank was an attractive man, he kept himself fit and barely had an ounce of fat on him. Though he was ten years older than Patrice, he didn't look like a man in his fifties. What had originally seemed refreshing about him, his commitment to personal grooming, coloring the gray in his hair, even having pedicures, had become subtly oppressive. She couldn't keep up, he expected the same standard from her which, for a woman, was much more demanding.

She kept focused on her image in the mirror, realizing that his anger was growing as she failed to grasp what the problem was. She didn't want an argument and wasn't about to be told what to wear. His patience disappeared. He grabbed her shoulders, pushing her forward until she was touching the glass.

"My wife is not going out in public with a fucking camel toe!"

She looked and even though she could kind of see what he meant; they looked no more revealing in that area than anyone else's did. Or did they? Did they look so bad? Was she about to make a fool of herself in public? If he could have said it in a kinder way, she may have been more open to listen, yet he had resorted to yelling at her. It felt like he was back to his old ways, and they were about to relive the very situation they had come here to leave behind.

Frank continued to rant. "I'm not coming to cheer you on if you plan to make a spectacle of yourself. I don't ask for much. How do you think this will look for me if you go out looking like that?"

He was, of course, being overly dramatic. She pulled at the fabric, stretching it and pulling down. What if she wore underwear beneath them? What could she wear instead? Patrice thought about how she got started running. She preferred aerobics or dance, yet she had put on a little weight and felt judged at those classes. It all seemed about wearing the studios branded gear and most of the women wore full makeup to exercise. If she was going to do a serious workout, her foundation wouldn't last five minutes. She went without make up once and felt like one of Cinderella's ugly sisters. She knew there were probably studios that were more relaxed but every time she tried one and didn't like it, she got a lecture from Frank. He even had ideas how her body should look, showing her women in magazines and telling how great it would be if she focused on a specific body part. He saw her experimentation with different forms of fitness as a lack of commitment and a weakness. Nothing had clicked before she started running.

Once she joined the original group and felt comfortable being outside, she loved it; it felt like she was completely free. Though she was glad in the end that her Pantheras had formed their own group. They had learned what they needed to put a program together and had fewer restrictions than being in a bigger, more formal group. She'd at first been reluctant. She'd worried they were too small. If one of them dropped out, they wouldn't have enough to support each other. It left them with Deb, herself, Lexi, sometimes Amanda and Nathan—yes, the strange guy seemed to want to be part of their group. He sometimes joined them on their training runs, and he and Lexi would often run ahead and have serious conversations. At first, she thought they were an item, though it turned out he was gay.

This group was more than running. It was the basis for friendships, and Patrice was grateful. Since marrying Frank, she had lost touch with her old crowd. Initially they visited or call, yet Frank's presence was always looming in the background, often disapproving, complaining after they left that they didn't like him, that she was choosing them over him. Eventually, they gave up, and it seemed easier than fighting it. Frank was right. She didn't need her old life. He had created a new one for her, although sometimes she worried about how much she had to rely on him. It was as if he wanted to be the only one that was close to her, though to be fair, he had encouraged her to run and that took her away from him regularly. These days it felt good to have something that was just for her, something that he couldn't control.

The group mostly met at Tea and Two. Most of the others lived close by, whereas Patrice lived further out of town. The gated community was on the outskirts of town in a beautiful valley overlooking the golf course. Frank chose it. He surprised her with the key code to the gate while they were still talking about moving. It overwhelmed her; how stunning it was, and it seemed ungrateful to say that she wished she could've been part of the decision. It was fully furnished and decorated; she didn't have to do a thing. But she enjoyed decorating, designing spaces had been her life before she met him, and it would've been a dream. She knew not to say anything. He could get really upset with her if she didn't see his point of view. And it seemed churlish and pathetic to be anything but grateful for such a wonderful gesture. He wanted her to be happy and to focus on their life together, not spend time on interior design and shopping.

She loved their home and especially the time she spent alone, reading with the warm sunlight streaming through the massive windows, and pottering around doing whatever she felt like. There was a different feel to the place when Frank came home. The first hour when she had to gauge his mood was often awkward, and sometimes if she had to admit it, she felt a little on edge. The drive to town felt like an escape, no cares, just time for her and her friends and a chance to run like when she was a kid. She was a little envious of the others as they got to hang out more.

Lexi seemed to live at the Volt and though much of it was part of her work, she also knew many of the regulars. She even knew the homeless people by name and sat chatting and doing jigsaws with them, although she seemed particular about the smell and sometimes wore one of those face masks. They didn't take it personally as she wore them a lot even when she was running. Frank would think she was weird. She wasn't someone you would bring home for dinner. In fact, there wasn't really anyone she would feel okay bringing home. Frank asked her about the group once, he seemed interested in Amanda, even though Patrice knew her the least. Maybe it was the minor celebrity bit he liked. Frank always said you should look for connections and how they could help your business. Patrice didn't care about all that and that is why, even though it made Frank furious, she refused to be part of the Tutus running group that he had encouraged, almost forced her to join. She put her foot down at being part of that snooty fake group of women. She wanted to be with people who would allow her to be herself, whoever that was. Sometimes she wasn't sure.

Patrice almost wore the leggings to spite Frank, but in the end had to admit they weren't the most comfortable around the crotch area. Wearing them to make a point, cutting off her labia to spite her face would be counterproductive. Frank planned to come to support her. She hoped he wouldn't. She didn't want his support if it was about control. It was as if a tiny warning light had shifted from the back to the front of her mind. Where it had glowed gently, it now flashed a little brighter and faster with every thought that included Frank.

The race number on her shirt and timing chip attached to her shoe made it all real. To the others, it may seem trivial, yet this was her thing, her group, her friends, and she would not let him spoil it. She'd been so desperately lonely and had almost given up hope of ever finding friends before meeting Deb and later the group. It was the turning point in her mental health struggles and the beginning of her renewed desire to be fit and well. It didn't matter how fast she ran; she hoped she could keep up because she was so scared of getting left behind or lost or doing something stupid. She was a runner, a member of a running club no matter how unofficial, and she had friends, real friends.

Her excitement gave way to worry. What if she needed to pee? What if she needed to do more than that? While everyone else would enjoy the buzz and anticipation that is almost tangible at a race start line, she thought about all the things that could go wrong. She was scared to carb load the night before, for fear of where she might have to carb unload. When Deb went on about toilet stuff, she pretended not to be worried.

She'd made the mistake of reading in depth about runner's toilet habit problems. The anxiety of a race, along with the body's sometimes unexpected response to running long distances meant that anything could happen. Maybe she should have ordered adult diapers instead of figure-hugging leggings.

With the number of cameras around, she could imagine being the first runner to go viral for pooping - *Poopy Patti takes a plop, Potty Patti couldn't wait.* Stupid headlines were floating around her head. The worst thing was, if she was honest, she was more worried about what Frank would say if she did anything to disgrace herself. Time to forget him and get ready.

10

They'd agreed to meet at the entrance to Tea and Two and walk to the start line together. Everyone else seemed to have had the same idea, and the café was crowded. It took a while for the group to find each other.

Lexi saw Patrice waving and noticed Amanda and Nathan standing with her.

Deb hurried to catch up. "Don't say anything, please?"

Lexi gave Deb a puzzled look. "Of course not." Turning to Amanda, she said, "Good to see you." Lexi knew that Amanda would have preferred to be running with them, rather than here as a "celebrity."

"Good to see you all. Hey if you see anything remotely interesting—wildlife related—take a photo with your phone."

Deb was perking up and joked. "I'm not sure I can spare the time. I'm aiming for elite athlete status today."

Nathan said "If you happen to use the potties, I dare you to take a photo of the state they are in, no-one will believe it otherwise. But no photographs under the bridges if people are pooping."

"Eww" Patrice was still not comfortable with all the toilet humor. "They don't really do that do they?"

Nathan put on his mock serious face. "I have known it for those who are serious about their race time, especially for the marathon. It mainly happens in the more prestigious races in big towns. The 10k route splits just before the big bridge, and that's where they would do it if they were going to."

Patrice narrowed her eyes at Nathan, then ignored him. She asked Lexi, "What is our game plan anyway, I mean I just want to finish and get the medal."

Lexi shook her head. "I'm sure we'll all stay together for the first few miles, though I'm not making any promises. If you guys stop at the beer stand, I won't wait for you."

"There's a beer stand? Hell I might just walk it after that!" They all knew Deb wouldn't. She was as excited as they were to be running the race.

As they walked over to the start line, they heard the thumping of the music and saw the giant archway that they would soon run through. As they lined up, Lexi felt uncharacteristically hyped. "Have a great race everyone. I'm proud of us for training through the hot summer months. This could be just the beginning, next stop half-marathon!"

Deb nudged Lexi. "Look, it's your buddies. Are we going to beat them?"

The Tutus were on the stage having photographs taken. They were officially the *Helping Hands and Happy Feet Running Club*. They were as annoying as they were overdressed, in the best matching gear with their own branding and accessories.

Patrice murmured, "You know my husband wanted me to join them?"

Lexi looked curiously at her. "You as a Tutu?"

"I know. Sometimes I don't think he knows me at all. He

introduced me to their leader, Celeste, at a Golf Club dinner, and she completely looked down her nose at me. He's impressed with the Tutu's charity work and that they are always in the news."

Lexi didn't mention that she knew Celeste in an official capacity, as she was keeping everything about her assignment to herself. She did feel safe commenting on what was common knowledge.

"She's a lawyer, right? I wouldn't want to hang with her either. She doesn't look like she'd be much fun."

Patrice, who rarely shared personal information or talked much about her feelings, was on a roll. "Celeste and the Tutus remind me of the bullies in high school. I have no intention of re-living that in my forties."

Deb said, "Amen to that."

"And her husband's a plastic surgeon. She had the gall to give me his card. Said if I wanted to hang onto a man like Frank, I should consider some fat melting treatments and get this? I should have started face fillers ten years ago."

Deb had seemed unusually quiet at the mention of Celeste and the Tutus. Though the last comment enraged her. "What? You're gorgeous! You don't need any of that."

Patrice looked like she might blush. "I've started to consider it to be honest, but I wasn't going to tell her that. I'm the oldest of us, you'll understand when you hit forty."

Lexi felt it necessary to correct her. "Actually, though Amanda is not running today, she's sort of one of the group, I believe she's in her fifties."

Lexi looked at the women on the stage. It wasn't unusual for runners to wear tutus at races, but they were over the top in their dazzling pink outfits with shiny pearlescent tutus. The mayor thanked them for all their *amazing* charity work and they did a twirl to display their t-shirts. Emblazoned on the front was the group's name. On the back were the words. "We run because we care."

Race mornings, although fun, could be tough. It was cold today and tensions were high. The Tutus had become a focus of the group's derision. Maybe they weren't individually bad people, but as a group, they were the perfect nemesis. Lexi wondered if they highlighted Deb's feelings of insecurity. Lexi had noted her self-deprecating comments that she guessed had a grain of truth, yet there was something else. The mention of Celeste's name had Deb on edge.

It would warm up as the race progressed. Yet right now, as Lexi was standing as close to the others as her personal boundaries would allow, she was grateful for the enormous man standing in front of her who acted as a windbreak. Patrice was motioning with her eyes for Lexi to look down before she whispered. "Look at his feet, he's forgotten his shoes."

Lexi wasn't sure if Patrice was joking. Maybe the barefoot running trend had passed her by. He was completely barefoot, though, not even with the protection of minimalist sandals some runners wore. She'd thought it was a fad that had come and gone. He was an interesting contrast with the others surrounding her, wrapped in trash bags for warmth.

Deb realized Lexi was shivering and had no extra layers. "Why didn't you bring an old sweatshirt?"

"I have nothing I am willing to throw away once I warm up. You might have noticed I don't have an extensive wardrobe. I prefer to shiver a bit and save the clothes I have."

Nathan had joined them, and he too was without extra layers. "In some towns, they collect the discarded trail of shirts, gloves and other layers that people toss. They clean them before donating to charity; as that doesn't happen here, I'm with Lexi. Being cold for a short time is the environmentally conscious choice."

Deb rolled her eyes as she wrapped herself further into her fleecy top and admired the old socks she was wearing as temporary gloves. "Well, you do you. I'm not freezing my butt off."

Lexi looked around to see who else she knew. She spotted Lorna, who looked every bit the elite athlete, even though she was almost twice Lexi's age. Lexi knew she wouldn't acknowledge her in public. Lorna took their confidentiality agreement seriously. Even if she was interpreting the rules more strictly than necessary, Lexi wouldn't jeopardize their working relationship by debating it. She needed Lorna. She'd helped rebuild her as a broken child. There was no one else Lexi could trust or could share her darkest fears with.

She was thinking about Zander; he was the first person she'd felt close to for a while, and she liked it. Part of her was waiting for the other shoe to drop. She wasn't fatalistic; she didn't believe because of her background that everything was bad, yet she knew there was always the possibility that someone was not who they seemed. She noticed supporters wrapped up warm, waiting, ready to cheer on the runners and wondered, what would it be like to have a family cheering her on? She realized if she could have anyone here it would be Remi, she wondered what he would think of Tribune. No, he would hate it, the pace would be too slow. She had a twinge of sadness and pushed the thought aside.

The Tutus had enjoyed their moment of glory, and now it was time for the mayor to make his self-congratulatory speech. Lexi seethed. She guessed that he was knee deep in the Volt plans. From information she had gleaned from meeting minutes and press interviews, he was no fan of the Volt and his opinions on the homeless community were less than charitable. He was probably getting a kickback from somewhere. The mayor concluded, and it was time for the anthem. A young girl sang her slightly tuneless rendition about as well as could be expected at such an early hour, and then they were ready to go.

The group beamed at each other as they heard the single shot of the starting pistol. The man without shoes was now hopping up and down on one foot. In the excitement of the push forward, someone had trod on his toe. What was that proverb about the man with no shoes? It needed updating, Lexi thought. The man who goes without shoes should practice social distancing.

Patrice was grinning as the group slowly made their way through the start line, among the hundreds of other runners. "I'm so happy to be running an actual race, I'm giddy I can barely believe it."

Lexi looked confused. "But you already did the 5K."

"Yes, but that was with the big group. We were spoon fed. This feels different. We planned our schedule and ran when no-one was telling us to. It feels like we've taken our training wheels off. Thanks Lexi, you kept us going."

Lexi laughed. "Would you like me to remind you of all the times I had to force you to run on Saturday mornings?"

Lexi looked around the crowd. She needed to find someone to pace. Someone a little faster than her, who she could keep up with until she pulled out all the stops and pulled ahead. She would wait until they got started and find someone. They had lined up in a relatively slow lane, so no one surrounding her would be suitable. She knew the others would want to chat. She planned to save all her energy for running. At the beginning of a race, there was always a mixture of types, kids, walkers, those in outrageous costumes, teams in matching shirts, those running to honor friends and family. As the race progressed, the numbers thinned out, and the runners became more serious and focused. They passed those with fun t-shirts with slogans.

*If you are behind me, you are too slow, and I'm just here
to make you look good.*

It always amazed her when she saw the elites returning,
having almost finished when mere mortals had barely got
started. The runners spotted Amanda and gave her a wave, just
as they realized Nathan had caught up with them. Deb said
what they were all thinking. "Aw crap, he really didn't register,
and he looks like he's planning on running with us."

If Nathan ran alongside the group and chatted, it gave the
impression that he was part of their team. Lexi felt awkward
and responsible. She would have to say something if he tried to
talk to her. She could try to outrun him, but he was fast. When
they came to the water table where local volunteers had
generously supplied baked goods and running nutrition, he
helped himself, not just to the water but handfuls of snacks. He
didn't care. Lexi skipped the water station and kept running.
She couldn't do this for all of them, but maybe she could lose
him. Nope, he was back with her before she had hatched a plan
to get rid of him. She could run more slowly, but hell no, she
wasn't giving up her chance of breaking her personal best time
because of him. She asked him in between breaths what the deal
was. "Why do you feel that everyone else should pay for your
race?"

"I'm not running a race; I'm simply running on a public
highway and generous citizens are giving out water and snacks.
The question should be why are you supporting a corrupt local
administration by funding services they already have a budget
for."

"I don't know if that's true."

He explained, even though she hadn't asked. "This race is
raising funds for charity, right? Including the free healthcare
clinic they offer at the Harbor. It already has allocated funds for

that; this just saves some money for them to siphon off somewhere else, probably for one of the mayor's vanity projects. No one wants to question donations to charity, so they get away with it."

Lexi was determined to keep up with him long enough to ask her questions. "I can see that you're trying to draw attention to corruption; it seems like an inefficient method if you have to explain your reasons to everyone individually."

Nathan gave her a wry smile. "I have other plans, I just want the people in charge to know I'm onto them."

As Nathan ran ahead, she saw what was on his shirt.

The lettering wasn't particularly big, but it got to the point.

Ask me how your entry fee for this race
is being used to support a corrupt council
and is stealing money from the charities
it claims to support.
I don't bite!

This guy means business, she thought, then realized he might be helpful. "There is probably way more shit going on in this town than you know."

Nathan slowed his pace slightly. "I'm listening. Though I know more than you think, we could probably help each other, we're on the same side. I'm here to throw them off the scent, while they think I'm the crazy guy who hijacks their race, they don't know that I'm looking into every corrupt deal that's happening in this peaceful little town."

Lexi was torn between asking him more questions and focusing on the race. She had no intention of telling him anything that could get her in trouble. She wondered if he really knew stuff, as he claimed and decided to test his knowledge. "So you know there's talk about closing the library?"

"That's not the half of it. I'm still trying to figure out what's going on but the people who were standing on the stage earlier, those who will throw a few dollars to a charity to look good, they epitomize what's happening in this town. There's something going on and it's not in the interest of people like you and me or those less fortunate."

Lexi knew instinctively that Nathan was genuine. His methods might be unorthodox yet she felt she could trust him. She shared her dilemma and explained the confidentiality and secretive nature of her work assignment without giving too many details, though it wasn't necessary. This guy was flying under the radar. They agreed to meet after the race to talk further.

As they ran through a neighborhood, well-wishers stood at the side of the road with signs.

You can do it.
Keep going, you're nearly there.

This was less than encouraging if you still had miles to go.

Running hecklers were a phenomenon that Lexi neither expected nor previously knew existed. The sight of women running brought out a strange urge for (mostly) men to yell random stuff. Many were just annoying, yet there was a good portion who were mean spirited. Lexi had at first tried to understand their reasoning. None of the group ran in dramatic, revealing or attention seeking outfits, not that those things would warrant the behavior. But the very idea of a woman using a public highway to exercise brought out a strange reaction from men in cars, on bikes, in their yards or even just walking by. Mostly, the words made sense just as the group was out of earshot, yet occasionally Lexi would fire off a quick-witted retort. In a small town, there was always the worry that you could piss someone off and Deb reminded her that some of these morons owned guns. Lexi wasn't concerned.

Some of the common comments were.
Run faster, fatso.
Fucking bitches!

Lexi ran as fast as she could. She broke her personal best and felt an emotion that was new. She felt *happy*. She'd enjoyed not just the running, but the camaraderie, the challenge, being part of something. She'd even managed to keep her thoughts off everything that might go wrong.

She might not have been as fast as she wanted to be but next time it would be better. Running to keep up with Nathan had made her faster. She hoped by the time they had a few more conversations, she would have even more to be grateful for.

Lexi waited at the finish line to cheer on the others. Deb appeared, not looking exactly victorious. It was a cool October morning, but Deb was sweating as if she'd ran a race twice the duration in midsummer. The events of the night before had taken their toll. Lexi passed her a bottle of water as she crossed the finish line. As they waited for Patrice Lexi realized she was standing next to a man she recognized. Though he didn't know her, she knew him. He had been at a meeting when the council had tried to sell off some land that was being used by the Learning Center and had spoken on behalf of the developers. He was full of his own importance. As Patrice passed the finish line and received her medal, he jumped in front of her and made sure the official race photographer caught him in the photograph.

Oh, so this was the famous Frank, he was *that* Frank. Patrice had not kept his identity a secret, but somehow Lexi had never connected her asshole with this asshole. Although Patrice was publicly positive about him, you didn't have to read far between the lines to see that there was something a little unhealthy about their relationship. Deb seemed to keep Lexi between her and Frank, and stayed turned away from them. It was if Deb didn't want him to notice her, though he wasn't paying her any attention. As Frank stepped forward to leave, Deb went pale and promptly threw up all over a tray of sliced oranges. Maybe the drug she took had an effect on her after all.

Patrice seemed suddenly oblivious to her friends. She'd said she wanted to hang with them, but Frank whisked her away before they had even given each other a high five. As Frank steered her in the direction of the VIP restrooms, Lexi saw him hand her a bag. He spoke loud enough for Lexi to hear. "Get yourself cleaned up and put these clothes on, you're a sweaty mess."

The Tutus lined up for more photographs. They had the fixed smile expression and an uncomfortable-looking pose as if they were models. Lexi would never understand those who craved a life that was all about being on camera. She'd spent her earlier years avoiding being recognized. Living a normal life was all she wanted. She was relieved to see that Tea and Two was not too busy. Most of the runners were still milling around eating the post-race food. She'd encouraged the group to meet for a debrief. Though even Lexi wanted to enjoy the feeling of victory for a little longer, the feeling of finishing a race, of achieving the end goal was like nothing else she could compare it to.

Deb and Nathan were doing selfies with her medal. Deb had regained her energy and motioned. "Come on, Lexi, we need you in this one."

Lexi was determined to retain her anonymity, and had to quickly think of an excuse, she shook her head, "I refuse to be associated with an unregistered runner. You should have got one with Patrice, though, and where is Amanda?"

Nathan was trying to figure out if Lexi was being serious about the photograph. "Last time I saw her, she was being dragged into the VIP tent. Shame no one got any good footage to save her job."

"Everyone did great, though we must remember we have another race coming up in just under a month and that is going to be tougher, lots of hills. We need to stay focused and do some weekend training in other areas that aren't so flat. Let's start back training on Tuesday, and I'll come up with a plan. Nathan if you want to join us, I want a commitment that you'll register."

"Well, the city isn't running the next one. So maybe I will."

Deb had replenished her lost breakfast with more donuts and wiped sugar from her mouth. "I need to use the bathroom. Lexi, I need to speak to you for a minute, don't leave before I get back."

Lexi wondered what Deb could want. She'd already agreed to talk with Nathan.

Nathan took this as his cue to leave. "I'll catch you another time."

Zander appeared. He placed a slice of his signature elderflower and lemon cake in front of Lexi. "This is from Deb. She apparently needs a favor and asked what your favorite item on the menu was. I can box it up if you don't want to eat it." Zander shook his head as he noted the donut sugar that covered the table. "She didn't even buy them here they're from the food trucks."

Lexi wiped a section of the table with a napkin and pulled the cake towards her. Deb returned and slid into the seat opposite.

"With everything that happened today and last night, I completely forgot that I was going to ask you something."

Lexi couldn't think what Deb could want, though she hoped it wasn't money. She felt guilty having the thought.

"I have to go away for a few days. It's my mom, she had a fall a few weeks ago. She had someone coming in to help but I found out she fired them. I'm going to sort it out and help until I get someone else. I need someone to watch my cats."

11

LEXI WAS UNMOVED as Deb pleaded with her. "I promise it will only be for a few nights. I have to leave tomorrow. You don't even have to touch them if you don't want to, but I've got to go, and I can't take them with me. My sister lives closer, but she's away on a cruise, she'll be back in a couple of days. My mom will probably be fine, but if anything happens to her, I'd never forgive myself."

Lexi remembered her visit this morning to Deb's place. The cat smell wasn't so bad, but the fur that drifted around attached itself to her clothes and stayed with her. The smell that bothered her was Deb's obsession with over-perfumed, chemically fragranced plug-ins and air fresheners. Had no one told her that this was no longer acceptable, not only being terrible for the environment but just tacky.

"Why did you leave it until the last minute? What do you normally do when you go away?"

Deb frowned. "I've only just found out. I've barely been anywhere in two years; I was married remember? There used to be two of us responsible for them and if we needed to his parents would..." Deb trailed off for a moment. "I knew it would be something I had to figure out if I wanted to go anywhere, I just hadn't got around to it."

Lexi immediately felt guilty, Deb so rarely talked about her life before she'd been widowed that Lexi had almost forgotten about it. "What would I have to do, I mean if you couldn't get anyone else?"

"You just need to come over, feed and give them fresh water, let them out, then lock them in at night, that's all, and I will be ever in your debt."

"Why can't you ask Patrice, she likes cats, she would probably enjoy it."

"I just can't okay; you are my only hope."

"Hang on, if I have to bring them in and then lock the cat-door overnight and let them out the next morning, that will be at least four visits."

"Oh, I guess you're right, well if they don't come straight back, you can leave them out. I just don't like the idea of anyone shoving stuff through the cat door when I'm asleep or away."

"I think you're being paranoid; I'll lock them in after they've done their business, but if they take too long, I'll leave the cat door open overnight, that's it, and before I come, you agree to dust thoroughly, vacuum, open all the windows to air it out and unplug all the chemical crap."

Deb was a little offended, "I'll write a list of instructions and I'll clean up; I promise."

When Lexi arrived at Deb's apartment as agreed she conceded that Bella and Blue were sweet cats, and she saw they could be pleasant companions.

Deb had attempted to de-chemicalize the apartment. Though Lexi noticed she hadn't put out the trash and they would pick it up the next day. Trash removal wasn't on her list of duties, but she couldn't stand to see it so full. Lexi immediately regretted her decision, papers dropped out of the kitchen liner as she removed it from the trash can. She looked around for rubber gloves and couldn't see any. While gingerly picking up the offending papers and dropping them back into the bag, a torn open envelope caught her eye. A check stub with a large figure peeked out of the top.

Her curiosity got the better of her, and she looked more closely. The check was payable to Deb from Fleming Research and Development for *Services Rendered* and was marked *Last Payment*. What the hell services was Deb providing that commanded this kind of payment? She thought about pocketing the stub before putting out the trash but it had remnants of food on it, she took a photograph. She would probably delete it later. It was none of her business, yet she had an odd feeling it might be important. Lexi had researched the pay rates in this town, they were pitifully low. She was fortunate that her skills put her in a well remunerated range. She knew from stories that Deb told that much of her better paid "consulting" was damage repair when Condo parties got out of control and needed emergency cleaning. They wouldn't pay nearly the amount on the check stub. Lexi told herself it was just further research on what was going on in the town, though she felt a flush of shame. She was breaking Deb's trust.

She stepped outside onto the tiny patio. There was little privacy, and it offered only a few feet of yard area. Bella was sitting still, watching for something. On further inspection, she saw Bella had already found what she was looking for but hadn't realized it yet. Less than an inch away from her nose was a lizard. Using its camouflage skills, it was the perfect color of the stone on which it sat. Lexi had heard that cats were smart. This one was letting the side down. It was friendly, though, and seemed not to care who was feeding it. Her brother Blue was less trusting and had decamped under the bed after doing what came naturally, without coercion.

Bella still hadn't done her business. Lexi wasn't entirely comfortable leaving the cat door open overnight. She would wait and give Bella a bit more time. So how long might this take she wondered?

Maybe she had time to call Remi? Which time zone was he in? She could never keep up. Was he currently on tour? He always took her calls unless he was on stage or in a television studio. They could go weeks without talking and as soon as they did, he was just Remi, the kid from The Sanctuary who she had loved like a brother, not the superstar that women even of her age would kill to have on speed dial. She looked out of the window and saw that Bella was now facing a low wall and staring at something that Lexi couldn't see. Okay, this was going to take a while.

Remi was the only person who she was happy to video chat with. They communicated far more than with just their voices. They'd built their close friendship on glances, codewords and secret signs. When Remi would speak to no one else, Lexi could disarm him with a glance. And when they wanted to share worries that The Sanctuary staff couldn't understand, they used their own language.

If he was still where he had been the last time they talked, it would be morning. He wouldn't mind if it was early. He was always telling her to call more often.

He picked up almost immediately. "Lex, how wonderful, pardon my mess, but I just got out of bed."

"Is there someone else in it? No, don't answer that. I have a test for you. Can you guess where I am and what I'm doing? If you guess correctly, I'll come out to meet you at a location of your choice like you keep begging me to."

"If you're prepared to do that, I presume it's something out of the ordinary and your comfort zone. I know it's not your place because there are some cushions behind you and it's not completely without color..."

"Cut it out, come with me, and the answer is." She pushed the phone under the bed, where Blue stretched out his paws lazily in Lexi's direction.

"No way you have a cat? No, that can't be right. I know, a crazy cat lady has kidnapped you. It's okay, I can pay the ransom."

Lexi explained her situation, and they spent a few minutes catching up while she monitored Bella.

Remi looked her in the eye. "Something's wrong. What aren't you telling me?"

"I have an assignment I don't know how to handle, and you know what not being in control does to me."

Remi spun around and showed her his apartment. Even from the small screen, she could see that it was gorgeous, with a stunning panoramic view of the city. "You don't have to do work you don't like. Come and work for me. You can be my assistant. I'll fire the one I've got, or just come and hang out. The guys in the band are okay but they're not my friends they don't know me like you do. No one does."

Lexi paused. "You know I can't do that. I still have stuff to deal with. Though I was thinking. I know you don't always get to decide where you play, but why don't you ever come here? There's a big arena not far away you could make it a mini vacation and come see me."

Remi laughed. "Lexi, have you ever seen the bands that perform there? There's no one under thirty. They come for their farewell tour. Look, if you are hanging around there because of Lorna, I could find you a better therapist. Lorna's great, but maybe it's time to try someone else?"

"You know it's not her, it's all me and hey I'm clearly making progress I'm currently watching a cat take a shit, that's not the action of an obsessive-compulsive clean freak who can't let go of the past."

"I can't do a show there but if you need me, if you need anything I will find a way. Just think about coming out, if not here then somewhere, there's a big, wonderful world waiting for you."

Lexi knew that Remi had mostly solved his issues, and he was no longer debilitated by them. She couldn't fool him and knew he worried about her. She didn't want him to know the truth, that sometimes she felt emotionally stuck, as if she were still in the room they had found her in all those years ago.

Lexi saw that Bella was now back in the apartment after doing her business. She said goodbye to Remi. It was always hard hanging up. Their bond had sealed something that was deeper than family, than friendship, or even romance. They'd saved each other. Even though they had both gone through the most awful experiences, they had eventually felt safe, even happy. Lexi had rarely replicated that feeling outside of The Sanctuary, until she'd found the Volt. She had to find a way to help save it.

12

———————

Lexi felt she deserved a break after going back and forth to Deb's in between working. She started with a strong coffee at Tea, then started on serious research at the library. She was used to getting her work done without distraction. The downside of finally having people in her life, was that took away her ability to focus. Though she had to admit some of her new favorite people were here.

"Lexi, come join me if you have a minute to chat." Amanda was sitting in a corner booth with a laptop and a pile of papers. Lexi looked dubiously at the only tiny space available to sit.

Amanda caught the look. "Let's move to the big table."

The round table in the middle of the cafe was the favored spot for the group and was feeling like the location of a secret resistance movement.

Amanda juggled what looked like the entire contents of her office as they moved tables. "So, what have you been up to? I haven't seen you around much this week."

"If I tell you, I don't want you to confuse me with any of your animal foster parents. I have been helping someone in need and this will be my last good deed for a while." Lexi filled her in on her cat sitting role.

Amanda listened while she organized her mobile office into neat piles taking up a third of the table. "I'm meeting Nathan for lunch soon; we can all have a catch up."

On cue, he came through the Atrium doors and waved as he went to order his lunch. Lexi gave Amanda a quizzical look, who responded with a grin. "You really need to get to know Nathan a little better, I think you'll find you've misjudged him."

Lexi was unconvinced. "Well, he annoys half the town and the other half think he's an idiot."

Amanda slid her laptop over to Lexi, which had a browser window open, displaying the online version of the local independent paper. It was a thorn in the council's side, especially the mayor. It took virtually no advertising, so was beholden to no one. The page was open at the column that offended, exposed, or annoyed anyone with power in the town. *Fly Guy, Private Eye.*

"He's Fly Guy?" Lexi's astonished expression was turning into almost excitement, and she didn't do excited.

Amanda gave her a wry smile. "If he was, he would be a good person to have on our side, right? No one knows for sure who runs the page or where the information comes from, but it's brought down a few leaders who learned that their connections couldn't always save them."

Lexi got the impression that Amanda was in no doubt who Fly Guy was and almost pleaded, "Oh come on. Tell me what you know."

Amanda closed the laptop and raised a finger to her lips. "I'm just here to protect the fishes and all God's other creatures. I can neither confirm nor deny any of your suspicions."

It seemed to Lexi that everyone was playing chess and pretending to play checkers.

Nathan joined them at the table. "Hey Lexi, as you are here, I think it's only fair that Zander joins us. I've told him to come over."

Zander brought over their drinks and sat at the table. "Is this the secret meeting of the People's Republic of Tribune?"

Amanda spoke quietly after looking around the room. "I hate to be the one to bring down the vibe, but things could be about to get serious for all of us. We need to lay our cards on the table and share what we know. Lexi, we know you are doing something that you can't talk about, but that doesn't mean that there aren't things that we can all discuss without you revealing anything. Saying all that, I'm not a lawyer. We'll keep you out of any meetings that could land you in trouble. I'll begin with the story so far: We know that there are plans to move the library. We can piece together enough evidence to believe that to be true. The Eden has mysteriously lost its funding and I am being offered the chance of starting a similar project at the other side of town. There's a council meeting scheduled that has an item about a change of use of a building that could be the Volt. We don't know anything definite about Tea and Two, the Entrepreneurial Center, or the Harbor."

Zander suddenly looked worried. "Well, there might be something. Lexi, remember the day I saw you downtown? I was on my way to the bank. They called me in. I've had a bit of a cash-flow problem and missed a few loan payments. I took on a big order for a private event and they wanted expensive food. Normally I ask for a deposit, but it was someone well known in the town, and she promised she would pay me. After I'd ordered the food they said they were no longer planning on running the event, no warning or apology. The order wiped out my savings and the bank have given me thirty days to pay. They're talking about calling in my loans. This could close me down."

Nathan looked puzzled. "So, you bought some expensive

food and have ended up stuck with it and the bill because they canceled. That seems suspicious. Surely you can threaten them with legal action?"

"Well, that's the problem. I know I've been stupid. It was all done verbally and get this; the woman placing the order was a lawyer. It's like she knew exactly how much would put me underwater and I wouldn't be able to do a thing about it. She said she was only asking for quotes not placing an actual order, which is a lie."

"This lawyer wouldn't be Celeste Collins, would it?" Lexi already knew the answer to her question. It was confirmed as Zander closed his eyes and nodded.

Nathan put his hand on Zander's shoulder. "I'm sorry Zander, you did the equivalent of clicking on an attachment in a scam email. It was a cruel, nasty move, but don't give up just yet. You've got good people on your side and we're working on the bigger picture.

Lexi scrolled on her phone and found the photograph she'd taken at Deb's. "Okay, guys, I have to swear you to secrecy because, I'm a little ashamed of what I'm going to share with you. I'm not normally a snoop."

Nathan said, "This whole meeting is sworn to secrecy and if you didn't already know, there is a rumor that I may or may not have a secret identity, so secret even I'm not sure it's me. What do you have?" Nathan was on the edge of his seat. He seemed to live for this stuff.

She showed him the image of the check stub on her phone.

"Yikes, what did you do to get hush money from those sleaze balls?"

"What? No, this isn't mine. I found it by accident at Deb's apartment."

"Then we might be in trouble. I know this company and

more importantly the man who signed this check and so do you."

Lexi put her hand to her mouth as she noted the signature and the company name, Frank Fleming, husband of Patrice. "I'm losing my touch, I can't believe I didn't connect the name."

Amanda looked at the photograph. "What's Patrice's husband paying Deb for? It wasn't a one-off payment. What type of service was Deb *rendering* that was worth the fee on this check, and why hadn't Deb mentioned she was working for Frank, you'd think it would have come up as she runs with his wife?"

Lexi said, "It's unlikely Patrice knew. They've never mentioned having any kind of relationship outside the group, and come to think of it, Deb has all but avoided Patrice recently. When I mentioned Patrice might feed her cats, she refused to consider it."

Nathan sighed. "I don't know, but whatever it is. It will be shady. Frank Fleming is good at keeping his hands clean. It won't be illegal, or he wouldn't be signing the checks."

Amanda looked up from her notes. "Someone is making sure they can choose to keep or dump whichever bits of the Volt they want, the earmark protection for the bequest of the money never made it into a document executed by the City Council. Frank Fleming is likely involved because he's a known property developer who has a history of dodgy deals."

Lexi felt completely out of the loop. "What am I missing about the Volt? What do you mean the protection's not in law? I thought the Volt was gifted to the city by a wealthy benefactor, I watched the video where he made the grand gesture, it was on the understanding that the money could only be used for that purpose."

Nathan had a resigned look on his face as he explained, "Though Ken Ferguson wanted to make sure that they could only use the building for the purpose intended, it needed legal paperwork that would take some time. He was keen for them to start the project, so donated the money on an honor agreement. Then he was tragically killed. The paperwork got kicked down the road. Ken wasn't there to insist upon it, and they'd already spent his money."

Lexi looked shocked. "That's crazy, so the city can do what it wants. Was there ever a question of foul play in his death? I mean the timing?"

Nathan nodded. "There were rumblings at the time that it might have been suspicious, but there was no evidence. Ken liked to walk at night. It was dark that night and there was no moon. Sadly, he wasn't found until the next morning, he might have survived if they'd got to him earlier."

Amanda looked upset, thinking about it. "He was one of the good guys, if someone did it on purpose... well I just can't imagine. We need to protect his legacy."

Nathan said, "Don't give up just yet. I'm following a couple of leads. There are some meetings happening around town that I'm pretty sure are part of all this. I need to get someone on the inside, someone who they wouldn't suspect of being involved in any resistance to the project. We need to know who's behind the sale. Even if hidden in a shell company, we must at least try to find out who's behind it. It's likely someone local's the connector. I know how these deals work, and I know people who can get me in. Let me try to see what I can figure out."

Lexi wasn't convinced Nathan knew what he was doing. Was he a loose cannon? Would he drop them all in it?

"I see that look, and I can promise you that nobody expects anything from me. I play the fool, and they think I'm a harmless nut. You have to trust me. We don't have a lot of time."

Lexi curled her lip. "I'm worried about people seeing us together there might be people watching, wondering why a random group is meeting. And as you are onboard, I know Amanda will have filled you in on my difficult position." Lexi whispered: "I'm supposed to be working for the other team."

"Well, we run together." said Nathan.

Lexi pushed, "But we don't include Patrice or Deb, and anyone in the know sees you two to be more political."

"Alright," Amanda conceded. "Let's keep meetings to a minimum. We can video chat when we all need to be together for now. You never know who might be listening. Nathan, can you use your contacts to see what you can find out about any new projects that link Frank to any of this? Lexi you promised to come over to the station sometime, I'm doing a live call-in show this week, I'll send you the details."

Lexi hadn't remembered promising anything, though she was secretly both delighted and terrified that Amanda wanted her to visit. A radio station was the last place she wanted to be, they broadcast the news, they had reporters. She silently told herself to get a grip, her story was almost three decades ago, she was worrying for nothing. No one here knew her or her past. In the little time she'd known Amanda, she'd grown to admire her and still held out the hope of them becoming friends. She had to stop herself imagining every scenario ending in doom.

Zander had left the table to serve a customer. Lexi saw that it was one of the Tutus ordering a latte—sacrilege, according to Zander. She was worried about him. He was doing his best, helping by keeping his eyes and ears open. He was perfectly placed to see comings and goings at the Volt. Though there was nothing as obvious as suits coming round with tape measures, there were definitely new faces appearing. They didn't look like they were there to check out books or drink tea. She barely knew Zander but couldn't imagine what would happen if he lost his business. Much like her, the Volt was central to his life. Lexi realized she was finding the emotional stimulus of so many new relationships a little overwhelming.

She needed to put her attention back to her work. Was there anything she hadn't considered? Could her unseen enemies be dangerous? Maybe she'd watched too many movies. This was not a town of gangsters, this was Tribune, where nothing much happened. Though maybe rocking the boat would change that. Lexi justified in her own mind at least that she hadn't disclosed anything to break the agreement. Though Celeste was clearly prepared to ruin Zander's business to get what she wanted, what might she do to Lexi if she crossed her? There was enough information already out there. In some ways, Lexi knew less than the rest of them. She had uncovered little in research. What was the big secret and why was the Volt so valuable that some would risk corruption charges to push it through?

Lexi stayed and drank more coffee. Less than a month ago, her life was settling into a happy rhythm. She needed calm, clean, and quiet. Could she book herself into The Sanctuary as an emergency? She could think of nowhere else that would be so calming. She had tried to replicate the serenity in her apartment, though the one thing it didn't have was a complete removal from real life.

"Bitcoin for your thoughts" Zander placed a tiny china plate with a fancy pastry in front of her laptop.

"Do you know how many ways your bastardization of that phrase doesn't work?" Lexi rolled her eyes while simultaneously sniffing the pastry before taking a bite.

"I am practicing my comedy routine. I'm thinking of having a stand-up night what do you think?"

"Please, sit down, and if you have time tell me something funny. I need a break."

Zander didn't need telling twice. "Okay well, we've never

had a comedy night, but did I ever tell you about how I almost got run out of town for hosting a play with full frontal nudity?"

She raised her eyebrows. "Please continue."

"In my eagerness to embrace all things Orwell, and before I realized no one was particularly interested, I hosted readings and performances of Orwell's plays. I was so excited to host a live dramatization of *Down and Out in Paris in London*. It was a big deal to get a New York company to come this far south, maybe they were on the run and heading to Mexico."

Lexi mock tapped her watch to keep the story moving and Zander continued.

"The play included a scene depicting Orwell as the victim of a robbery, losing even the clothes he stood in. The theater group's commitment to authenticity meant the scene ended with the actor playing Orwell frozen in place—completely naked."

Lexi gasped and then laughed, imagining this happening in Tribune.

"In cosmopolitan cities, productions such as this would be a huge hit. In Tribune, a penis in spotlight was not a usual or welcome sight. Thankfully, the Church Women's Guild did not attend the performance. Though the Trib featured a review suggesting sausage sandwiches as a new British menu item."

Lexi wasn't sure if he was joking. "I'm going to look up the review to see if this is a true story!"

"Comedians often make fun of people's names, so tell me your actual name. Lexi, I'm officially Alexander and though Xander would be the proper shortening of my name, I refuse to have a name beginning with an X."

Lexi laughed. "Well, don't worry, I have your X I'm officially Alexandra."

"Shit, no way! I never even considered it. We have the same

name. We are the same person destined to meet, two halves of the same whole, yin and…"

"Hmm, Alexander, if that's part of your routine you need to work on it."

"Then allow me to be serious. I always enjoy your company. I know you like to keep yourself to yourself, but if you ever wanted some company that wasn't with the local hacker, drug-dealer or shady politician, I always have comp tickets to the Theater as they leave all their flyers here."

"Drug-dealers?"

"So I heard."

"Who? Oh, never mind. You obviously have received sullied data. I'll make a deal with you. If neither of us is homeless nor in jail in a month's time, I'll come to the theater with you."

Lexi knew that a month was a long time, yet saying it aloud felt like a commitment, she didn't say things she didn't mean. She felt a shift, as if she was finally ready to risk being vulnerable in the pursuit of connections.

Zander collected her plate and espresso cup and returned to the coffee bar with a spring in his step.

13

LEXI TRIED to think of reasons why she shouldn't visit Amanda at the radio station. Yet in the end pushed herself to go. If the Volt closed, she would be back to spending all her time alone. She needed to solidify these new relationships. She struggled to admit, even to herself, that she needed people. She'd survived without them for so long, and since leaving The Sanctuary on the rare occasion she'd let her guard down, people had disappointed her.

The station was in a strip mall in an area that Lexi was unfamiliar with. Though it wasn't far from her apartment or the Volt, it was in a less salubrious area of town. She realized she didn't venture out very far, she limited her life to a half a dozen square miles and knew little of what was beyond. It was as if she was recreating her version of The Sanctuary, a safe space where no danger or risk would be allowed in.

Lexi peered through a tinted window to make sure she was in the right place. Amanda saw her arrive and came out to greet her. "Lexi, you found us! Come in. I'm sorry if my description of a 'station' led you to believe it was anything fancy. No one can see us on the radio. Have you done any radio before by the way?"

Lexi laughed. "I'm not here to do any radio, am I? And no, unlike you Amanda, I like to be inconspicuous."

Amanda groaned. "You know I'm just playing the game. Sit over there, put on those headphones and you'll see how it works. It might help you direct the group to what is and isn't a good call. Maybe we will get a sighting of the Trib-Trib Tiger. I still can't get my head around the fact that our town of Tribune's local newspaper that could have chosen a Gazette or an Echo, decided on a Tribune. So yes, the Trib Trib Tiger seems to have stuck."

Lexi was finding this less serious version of Amanda refreshing and charming. Though she wondered what she had to be happy about with all that was going on.

"Oh, and this is Ted. Ted meet my friend Lexi. Ted is both engineer and sometimes, co-presenter. He helps weed out any callers that might be dangerous."

Lexi only had a moment to enjoy the unexpected pleasure of being described as a friend, as she registered the last word. "Dangerous?"

"We have to find a balance between spicing up the show and putting Amanda in danger." Ted said.

Lexi was processing this information when they signaled it was time to go on air.

Amanda gave her a reassuring smile. "We can talk during the commercials."

With the jingle and preamble done, Ted was ready to introduce the first caller.

"Amanda, we have Jimmy on the line and he has a question about what he thinks might be a genetically modified bird."

"Okay, go ahead Jimmy, what do you have?"

"Well, I was looking up at the sky before I closed the blinds and put my security spikes out and I see these birds and they were swooping, and I got to thinking they might be spy birds. Me and the government don't see eye to eye and I'm pretty much off the grid, so maybe they're sending them to spy on me."

Amanda looked at Ted and shook her head. "Well, Jimmy, I'm not familiar with spy-birds. Do you have a photograph for me so I can identify which species they might be using?" She was being deliberately sarcastic, but the guy didn't seem to notice. He probably normally tuned in to the conspiracy shows. Ted was already on it and forwarded her a video that Jimmy had sent. They insisted on this to weed out the time wasters.

"We'll go to a break while I take a minute to look at the evidence. Jimmy, stay on the line."

Lexi was beginning to understand the world that Amanda was inhabiting and the potential for things to turn sour. Amanda seemed to enjoy it.

She came back to the call where Jimmy was still waiting. "Well Jimmy, you were right. These are definitely not common nor garden birds they are, in fact..." Amanda paused for effect. "These are bats Jimmy, you have a yard full of bats. I zoomed in, but I couldn't see any cameras in their eyes. Now don't you go shooting them, because they're a protected species."

Ted was gesticulating for her to cut the call. As it dawned on Jimmy that she was making fun of him, he became angry. "You don't know what you are talking about you--" thankfully the seven second delay meant that the audience didn't hear the racial slur that he yelled at her before they cut him off.

"Well, that was Jimmy proving that he's probably got a lot of bat shit happening over there." Amanda quipped. "Now we have a new segment and this time Amanda will ask you. We have a rich variety of wildlife right here in Tribune and we'd like you to see if you can find some of the less common ones. Now we don't want anyone to disturb wildlife that you come across, however if you see any, we'd like you to take a photograph and send it in. You must of course do this safely and they must be live animals. If you would like to take part, we are offering a prize for a good quality photograph of the critters on the list. You can find it by going to the website or our Glass Jelly page and it will also give you a handy map to show you the areas you are most likely to find them. The first good photograph I see will win a pasta dinner. Yes, I'm offering a gift card that will feed a family of four at our very own *Basta Pasta* restaurant. So, get outside, get some fresh air and send me your photographs."

Amanda took off her headphones and displayed a wry smile as Ted came into the studio.

"Amanda, we don't have a budget for prizes we barely have a budget for you. What are you playing at?"

She swiveled around in her chair. "Don't worry about the prizes, we've got enough freebies, the college will fund some, and the gift card is mine. Lexi have you eaten at that God-awful restaurant? I promise not to give you freebies from there. Hey let me show you the website Nathan created for the Ask Amanda page. He even has bird recognition software. I don't know where this will go but at least we have people interested in wildlife again."

The website was impressive, though Lexi was becoming anxious about how long they'd been talking. "Are you still on a commercial?"

Amanda laughed, "We're right on time, put your headphones back on."

Ted gave her the signal and she was back on air.

"And it seems like we have some interest already in our new Tell Amanda segment. Hello Princess what do you have for us?" Amanda tapped Lexi, alerting her that something was about to happen.

"Hey there Miss Amanda, yes this is Princess and we got

ourselves a live one over here. I think I saw one of these on a sci-fi show. It's got armor plating and everything. My boyfriend says it's an Amarillo, though to be honest I thought they were extinct."

"Can you send us a picture real quick?" Amanda mouthed "Deb," to Lexi.

"Sure, give me a minute."

Lexi almost didn't recognize Deb's voice, she was hamming it up so much.

"Yes, that is an armadillo. It looks like a car hit it. It's probably dead, but don't move it yourself. Some may carry leprosy."

Deb aka Princess, let out a shriek. "What? Leprosy? Like in the Baarrble kind of leprosy?"

Amanda was now biting her lip to stop herself from giggling. "Things have moved on since those times and it's treatable these days, but you still shouldn't touch it. We'll get someone out to clean him off the street."

When the show was over, Amanda drove Lexi back to her apartment and they walked to a bar for drinks. "So, what do you think? Admit it, Deb is funny. She comes up with random stuff spontaneously and the listeners love her southern drawl. I'm never sure if she's being real or not."

Lexi paused before she answered. "I can see that the show could grow into something that people will enjoy and learn something from, but what Ted said about it being dangerous for you, do you get a lot of the racist stuff?"

Amanda took a long drink of her wine. "You notice I didn't choose to have a drink near the studio. I don't hang around after my show, because you never now. People think free speech means they can say what they want and, unfortunately, the racists are saying what many people are thinking. Ted's heart is in the right place, but he wants me to go out of my way not to offend people, to be polite when dealing with assholes. He thinks then they won't have an excuse to attack me. They never need one. I'd rather let them crawl from the woodwork and out themselves. The guys who present the other shows don't take shit and neither will I."

Lexi realized how little she knew or understood living in her privileged bubble.

"And Lexi, I have to be honest and say the reason I started running with you guys was to placate my husband. He worries about me being out on my own, especially at night. I told him I'd joined a group. I mean you are a kind of, sort of group, right? Even though I just tag along sometimes."

Lexi laughed, "Sounds like we both ended up in the group by force. I'll fill you in on my story another time."

Amanda nodded. "I'm glad though, in a way. It's good, the idea of having a group of friends again. I lost most of mine moving here. Nathan's the closest thing I've got and most of our stuff is about work. Do you consider the group as your friends?"

"Can't say I've anything to compare it to but... maybe. I'd like to think so."

Lexi sensed that Amanda wanted to probe deeper and she wasn't ready for it. She jumped back with her own question. "What about the women at the fundraisers and dinners? I've seen you with some of them, in photos I mean?"

"Oh God, no, they're not my people. Their charitable work always includes an abundance of champagne, cocktail dresses and thousand-dollar shoes. I don't fit in for many reasons, and not the obvious one. I'm incapable of holding a fake smile for longer than it takes to snap a photo."

"And Nathan, how do you know each other, I mean how did you meet? Does he work for you?"

Amanda smiled. "Nathan and I just kept meeting at events and finding ourselves on the same mostly-losing side of battles.

We found we had similar values and we come together to do what's right when it's needed. He's kind of Tribune's superhero. He is one of the smartest, most resourceful and kindest people I know, and I'm not even sure if I should say what I am about to say out loud."

Lexi's eyes widened, waiting for what would come next.

"I'm married and I love my husband, yet he can be protective and a little jealous, it helps that a man I spend a lot of my time with has no romantic or sexual interest in me, and not just because I'm almost two decades older than him."

Lexi was grateful that Amanda had opened up and hoped she would feel comfortable in sharing her secrets at some point. They finished their drinks and headed out.

"I hope today was useful, let's meet again soon. Let me know if there's anything you need help with."

Lexi had enjoyed the day more than she had hoped. Now she didn't know how to end it. The very idea of hugging made her shrivel inside and even if she could force herself to, it would be awkward. Amanda was almost a foot taller than her. Shaking hands would be weird. She settled for putting her hands in her pockets and then raising her arm as she walked backwards. She knew she'd replay this scene later and torture herself with her lack of social graces.

14

Lexi thought all weekend about what else she could do to save the Volt with the constraints she was working under. This was the first time she felt like her work mattered, and she was supposed to be working for the other side. Too many people's lives would be affected if she messed up. She plotted everything she knew on a whiteboard in her home office. She had gone down a rabbit hole, looking into Frank Fleming.

When she wanted to get a true picture of someone, she often uncovered the most useful information by joining chat rooms or reading forums. Though there was nothing official that she could prove, there was chatter, people feared him, he was implicated in a nasty and sometimes violent activity, though none of it had stuck. Much of what she read was anonymous, yet she was building a picture of a very different man from his public persona. Handsome and sharp-dressed, a youthful looking fifty, he was the poster boy for small town self-made success. This image was not shared by those who got in his way. It took Lexi hours to follow the threads. Some stories were third hand and could have been dismissed as rumor, but they told a similar tale. People who crossed him were threatened, tied in legal knots, too afraid to speak out. He ruined lives, withheld payments, and when he could get away with it, according to many commenters he found other more brutal ways to come after them.

Lexi struggled to believe that Patrice was married to such a man, yet there were too many similarities in the accounts for it to be all gossip. And then there was Deb. What did she know? Was she doing something illegal for Frank? Lexi wasn't sure what she was going to do, but she needed to do something. A text message seemed like the easiest first step.

> *Hey Deb, do you have any free time today? I have some research to do at the library and wondered if you could help with a bit of local history? I'll be there around 2:00 pm.*

A Sunday seemed a good day for a conversation without too many people being around to eavesdrop. Deb responded almost immediately.

> *Sure, I owe you after you saved me with the cats. I'll see you soon.*

As Lexi was preparing to leave, she heard the unmistakable ringtone she'd assigned to Remi's calls. He'd told her when they last spoke that he'd be checking in regularly and if she didn't respond he would send someone to do a welfare check. Though he was half joking, she knew he was worried about her, so she answered. "Remi how are you doing and why can't I see you?"

Remi turned on his video. "Look it's daytime I'm getting closer to you, I'm even in your time zone."

Behind Remi was a blue sky and palm trees, he knew that this no longer impressed Lexi so didn't bother trying.

"Are you stalking me? I mean you were at the other side of the world a week ago. Though seriously it's good to see you."

Remi crinkled his eyes in a way that would make a million teenagers swoon, yet this look was only for Lexi. "What's happening? Have you solved your dilemma? I know you've been fretting."

Lexi packed a bag with her laptop and notepads as they talked. "I'm still working on it, and I hate to do this but I'm actually heading out now to follow up on something. Can I call you later or let me know when's the best time? You can call off the welfare check people."

Remi didn't look happy to let her go. "Lexi I can tell things aren't right with you—look at me, I want you to hear this. I can get to you within a few hours. I have resources. Nothing would stop me from coming to you. If you need anything, I better be the first call you make."

Lexi nodded. She knew that if she asked, he would do as he promised, though it might come at professional cost. She couldn't do that to him. If she had shared what she had discovered about Frank, Remi wouldn't be happy.

Lexi thought a walk would help her think about what she would do next. She took a scenic route through the park and along the waterfront, then sat for a few minutes, the welcome breeze blowing through her hair. As she closed her eyes, she allowed herself a minute of peace, hoping an answer would come to her. She felt a little guilty that not all the running group were in the loop about the drama that was unfolding in between meetings. She had to decide about Deb. Did she confront her? What if she was part of some dodgy dealings with Frank connected to the Volt deal?

She almost wished she hadn't seen the check stub. It meant she didn't know if she could trust Deb if she needed her. Could Deb and Patrice be having secret meetings, too? She'd finally found people she liked, she would be so disappointed if she was to find that she'd been wrong about them. Deb often lingered after their meetings, claiming to have nothing but time on the weekend. She seemed to have a lonelier existence than the others. Lexi realized how little she knew about any of her new friends. She needed to remedy that if they were to begin meaningful friendships, and eventually let them know her. She would give Deb the benefit of the doubt and see where it led her.

It was a beautiful day, and most people were outside enjoying the sunshine, eating at the food trucks, or sitting by the water. Tea and Two was almost empty.

"Hey Lexi, I rarely see you on a Sunday. You are just in time to try one of my new creations." Zander was assembling the pieces of tiny individual pastries. They looked like 3D representations of the Volt with the Atrium roof in different colors of icing.

"They are amazing, though I can't imagine you could make any profit on them. They must take forever."

"They're not for sale. He presented a much larger version that had the words. "Save the Volt" iced on the side as if it was written in graffiti.

"Zander you can't do that, no one is supposed to know."

"And they won't yet. This is just practice, but we need to think of ideas to raise the profile. If we are right, we might not have much time."

"Put it away. I'm meeting Deb, she'll be here in a minute."

Deb arrived soon after. The tray of smaller cakes were still sitting on the counter.

"Coffee and a Volt Cake?" Zander asked.

"Wow cool, you must have too much time on your hands. If they taste as good as they look, I'll take one."

Lexi found a booth. She wished Deb hadn't seen the Volt

cakes, the mess she would surely make would disturb Lexi and she needed to focus. She wasn't sure how to start the conversation.

Deb jumped in while she was still thinking about it. "Lexi, I'm glad you asked me to come. You've seemed distant since you looked after the cats. I wondered if I'd offended you?"

Lexi knew her next move could be disastrous for her, but she needed to know what Deb was working on that could be so lucrative and for a power player like Frank. "Deb, I work with projects that are highly confidential, and anyone I work with has to be completely trustworthy. If I was ever to share information with you, I need to know I have complete discretion."

"Hey, I don't just clean condos and help with people's errands. I get some pretty top-secret shit sometimes but, of course, I can't tell you about it."

"Right and that's why I have to be sure that there wouldn't be a conflict of interest if I was to share any information about my work."

Deb looked puzzled.

"I need to know what kind of work you do for this company?" Lexi showed her the photograph of the check stub that Deb had received from Frank's company.

"Where did you get this? Did you go through my things?" Deb's face went from bright red to deathly pale, and before Lexi could come up with her prepared explanation, Deb covered her face and crumpled into a sobbing mess. This was not what Lexi had expected. "Who sent you? Is he spying on me? Is Patrice working for you?"

It was Lexi's turn to be confused. She waited until Deb was calmer before continuing, "The pay stub dropped out of your trash as I was emptying it. I admit I was nosy. Frank, he's not a good person for you to be working for."

Deb looked at her through desperately unhappy eyes. "He's

not, and I'm scared of him. I did something I regret, and I don't know how to make it right."

Lexi sat back and relaxed. "Deb, I have all afternoon. I doubt telling me will make it any worse, and it's even possible I can help, once I know what's going on."

Deb blew her nose, took a sip of her coffee, and prepared to tell Lexi her story. "It all started with an ad I saw in the Trib, it was just after Christmas. I'd promised myself I would try some new stuff, so when I saw the ad, I went for it. It might help you to see it. I took a photo. I sent it to my sister in case it was some weird human trafficking thing. Hang on while I find it. January —Okay, here it is." Deb handed her phone to Lexi.

Running partner required for beginner female runner.
Three-month commitment.
No running experience required.
Confidentiality essential.
Generous allowance.
Send resume to PO Box below.

Lexi didn't know what she was expecting, but this wasn't it. "So, you went for an interview. Where does Frank come in?"

"The interview was where it all began. It seemed like easy money and was mysterious enough to have piqued my interest. I wondered, of course, who wants a running partner who doesn't run? Well, I ran a bit and so thought why not give it a whirl. I wasn't too worried. I thought it was probably an overweight executive who wanted to get fit and didn't want anyone to know, though I couldn't guess why wouldn't they just hire a personal trainer. I sent my resume to the PO Box and received a reply that included an application form with a confidentiality agreement. It all seemed strange.

"I've done some weird jobs in my time, and I've learned to

be cautious and go with my gut instinct, but there was nothing that seemed too worrying. I dressed conservatively for the interview, clothes that would allow me to run from a potential serial killer and not too revealing in case it was a pervert. You wouldn't have recognized me with my hair in a low ponytail. I even wore reading glasses. I guessed I could probably pull it off for about five minutes before I said something inappropriate or dumb. You know me Lexi, I'm not the most serious person, and it was all feeling like I was on some reality TV set up."

Lexi wanted her to get to the point but could see that Deb felt it was important for her to know the entire story.

"The interview was at the new tower block downtown, the one with its tall sides of glass and steel."

Lexi's ears pricked up. "The one that had the issue with planning permission. It was higher than was supposed to be allowed for the area?"

Deb nodded. "It was on the local news there'd been a protest, but it didn't come to anything. Anyway, I go where they said to go. I don't have a name to ask for and there wasn't a receptionist, just a fancy, expensively furnished waiting area with a full-size window overlooking a park. Two other walls had fish, lots of them; colorful fish in tanks sunk into the walls like moving art installations. I waited and felt like a fish myself, like I was in a tank, and someone was watching me. Without warning, a door I'd not noticed before, slid open and what had been a solid wall now had become glass. I'd seen this stuff on TV but didn't think it was for real. Whatever this job was, I wanted it.

"Sitting behind a desk in an office the size of my apartment was a man. He saw the look on my face. He got up and he's like hey, 'I guess I'm not who you were expecting? Don't worry, the job is to work with my wife.'"

"Right there, that was it, the moment I should have walked away. There's always a moment when you get to decide. You see it on those TV shows where someone's asked to carry a package onto a plane, just before they do it, that little voice gets louder it tells you 'This a is a bad idea.' And you think no, it'll be fine. I won't get caught. When they are in the hell hole prison far from home, they remember that voice. That was my moment. I chose wrong. The classy office, the big paycheck. I convinced myself it was all going to be okay."

Lexi asked. "So, it was Frank?"

"He told me loved his wife, but she was becoming needy, isolated, and unhappy. They had moved here for his business interests, and she had given up what she knew and loved in New York. Reading between the lines, he seemed more concerned she might embarrass him. She'd put on a little weight, he was worried she was turning into someone he couldn't show off at the Country Club. I wasn't sure if he cared for his wife, or was just a manipulative asshole. Remember, I didn't know him, and he was putting a good spin on it. Every time I was ready to say no, he would claim this was a way to help his wife make friends. Once she was established in a running group, I could back off and allow her to develop her own friendships. He had it all planned out. He wanted me to join the 5K group. His wife was already planning on joining. He needed to make sure that she stuck with it. I would run with her, introduce her to people, and stay with her until she was settled, until her first race. I wasn't sure I could do what he was asking. In the end I figured I'd nothing to lose. Then it got real. He brought in a lawyer who explained the confidentiality agreement.

Lexi was ahead of her and wondered why this woman was in everything, "Celeste Collins, leader of the Tutus and all-round nasty piece of work." Lexi wasn't ready to share that she knew plenty about Celeste, not yet, but it made sense that she was working for Frank.

"That's her, and now you know what I do for Frank. I wish I didn't. I'd like to pretend it never happened. I like Patrice a lot, and there's no reason that she should ever know. But Frank, he won't let me go and keeps insisting that I do other jobs for him."

"Are you not worried about breaking the agreement?"

"Well, are you going to tell anyone? And I think we're beyond that now, he's threatening to tell Patrice and twist it somehow, though I think I have enough dirt on him to cause him more trouble than he can make for me."

"What other jobs, what is he asking you to do?"

"Just random running around for him, but enough for me to see he's connected to some sketchy people."

"Deb, Patrice deserves to know who she's married to. It won't be pleasant, but you need to tell her. I'll try to help you, but I need you to tell me everything you know about Frank, every detail and everywhere you've been and who you've met with on his behalf, and then I'll tell you a little of what I know. But first tell me, why did you keep running with us? Wouldn't it have been safer to walk away?"

"We'd become friends. You understand, I think. They're not easy to find. I'm sorry, but I know you're keeping your own secrets. I know there's something going on that the rest of you aren't telling me. I see you all whispering."

Lexi was furious on Deb's behalf. "Let's stay focused on you for a minute. Frank's been socially engineering Patrice's life and now is trying to blackmail you. It makes sense why you've avoided some of our group activities. I'd also noticed you were uncomfortable at the mention of Celeste's name. Frank has managed to not only gaslight his wife, but he's also done a number on you. Tell me how it worked out from the beginning?"

Deb furrowed her brow, "At first it was what we agreed, a straightforward 'Buddy' job, then he started to change the rules, he wanted me to keep an eye on Patrice, he wanted to know who she talked to the most. We were supposed to be done after the race, but when he realized we planned to continue running together he saw it as an opportunity to keep using me. I tried to break off the agreement, but he said he'd tell Patrice. Then he wanted to know about you all."

Lexi's face dropped. "Us, me?"

"Not you specifically, all of the you. Frank was keen to know about Nathan, if he was part of the group, what he talked about. Then he started asking about Zander. He was weirdly jealous."

Lexi relaxed a little. "What did you tell him?"

"Well, it's not like I know much, and he kept bugging me so, I, well I kind of made stuff up."

"I don't like the sound of this. What exactly did you tell him?"

Deb had got over being upset and had gone back into her default droll mode.

"None of us know much about you so I thought a background in the circus would be a good fit, not the old-fashioned kind, you know the ones with hot trapeze artists, I could see you doing that."

Lexi didn't know whether to laugh or be mad at Deb. "Maybe he'll avoid me if he thinks I can breathe fire. What else?"

Deb said. "Well, he was being rude and snarky about Nathan, I guess Patrice told him he was gay, that seemed to bother him, so I gave him something to think about, I said we all thought he was undercover FBI."

Lexi let out a loud. "Ha! He'll love that." She realized that for all she knew he might well be. "Anything else?"

"He didn't seem worried about Amanda; they move in similar circles so she's not a stranger like we are. I just gave him enough to shut him up until the next time he asked. He didn't just have me doing stuff related to Patrice, he had other jobs and when I was uncomfortable about them, he would say it would be the last one."

As they talked, Zander caught Lexi's eye. He raised his eyebrows and mouthed, "You okay?" He had seen the initial emotional outburst and had been monitoring the proceedings while polishing the same coffee cup for the last twenty minutes. Lexi gave a nod of the head. There would be time to fill him in later. He wasn't fully up to speed on all the latest shenanigans either.

Lexi wasn't sure what she could do to help Deb's situation. She needed to find out what Frank's involvement in the Volt scheme might be. The only person who didn't seem aware that Frank was up to no good was Patrice. This could backfire spectacularly if she discovered half a story. Deb was going to have to be brought into the plan, not that they even had one yet.

Deb had gone back to feeling down. "You guys keep me sane. I hoped it would all go away, and I could forget it, but Frank seemed to enjoy having a hold over me."

"It also gives him a hold over his wife, even if she doesn't know it. Wouldn't you like to turn the tables on him? He's up to some shady stuff. You want to help expose him?"

Deb frowned. "I don't know that I could do it. I'm trying to get myself out of trouble not in more of it."

Lexi's face hardened, and for a fleeting moment she let Deb glimpse a side of her that most people never got to see. "You have deceived all of us for months. Maybe you can put that skill to good use for once. Though first, you need to make things right with Patrice."

15

<hr>

LEXI AGREED to meet Nathan at the Volt before the Council meeting. It was quiet early in the evening. There would be hardly anyone around and it was unlikely their meeting would raise too many suspicions. They hoped they might discover something new at the Council meeting.

"Nathan, I found out the truth from Deb. She's been working for Frank, though she knows nothing about the Volt, and she's in over her head." Lexi gave him a much shorter version of Deb's story.

Nathan looked worried. "It's clear Frank knows you are connected to Deb. You need to know this. Frank Fleming is a dangerous man."

"I know, though I'm not sure what to do with that information Nathan."

"Just be careful, If anything out of the ordinary happens let me or someone know. Frank is not against using dirty tricks, even violence, to get his own way."

They left to attend the meeting. Nathan suggested to Lexi they sit separately. She arrived first and sat at the back. She knew Nathan had some tricks up his sleeve. These meetings attracted a certain level of crazy. Nathan's kind of crazy. He banked on the idea that they would dismiss him as the type of nut job who showed up and wasted everyone's time. This was, he claimed, part of his cover story to keep them from knowing what he was up to. Lexi suspected he also did it for the hell of it. She wasn't sure she would be able to keep a straight face. It would have been good to sit with him so he could at least keep her awake, but they needed to keep their distance, at least for the next few weeks. She remembered the council recorded the meetings. She had to avoid catching his eye.

The level of dullness was astounding. She couldn't wait for him to spice things up. Everyone could have their say if they wrote their question or point down in advance.

When it was Nathan's turn, he leaned into the microphone and brought forward his proposal. "Good people of Tribune, I see that many of you are of a religious persuasion. I noted your bowed heads during the invocation, and I also know you are firm believers in the Constitution."

There were rumblings of agreement as he continued. "My first responsibility is to draw your attention to the First Amendment's Establishment Clause. I'm sure you all have a copy at home so I will summarize. The clause prohibits government actions that favor one religion over another or over preferring religion over nonreligion. I've not yet seen an invocation from an Atheist or Buddhists, neither a Pagan nor Muslim. As I'm not a member of those beliefs, I cannot speak for them, however I would like to propose my religion to take its rightful place to lead the prayer at the next meeting, and permission for distributing literature on Sundays."

Someone shouted, "What religion?"

"The Wheel of Judgement is a faith that worships the wonder that is the Wheel. The Wheel was the turning point on which civilization formed. We worship the wheel and all things circular; the Prayer of circular and perpetual motion will be a wonderful start to any meeting. We propose that we be allowed to stand with our brethren from all the other religions. It seems only fair that we be given the same opportunity to harass the heathens and tourists that they enjoy every weekend. Us "Wheelies" as we like to be known, also believe in supporting our unhoused brothers and sisters. This council has banned the homeless from standing on street corners with their signs, surely, they have as much right to their freedom of speech as some of the zealots who are the reason online review sites claim Tribune is full of bigots.

As the jeers from the public gallery grew louder, Nathan brought his monologue to a close. Among his satire he had some serious points. It left the council members blustering in indignation. They didn't know how to deal with someone like Nathan. They refused to grant him the right to distribute literature of his own new religion—not that he had any intention of taking his pointed joke any further. They could not refuse him the right to lead a future meeting in prayer, and it upended the meeting in confusion. It was fun to see him tie them in knots with his arguments. Nathan's eccentric reputation was solidified. It would help create a smokescreen separating him from any connection to the Volt closure.

Lexi noticed Amanda slip in during his talk. She had piles of documents with her and looked deep in thought. Lexi hoped they could catch up after the meeting. The motion they were waiting for came, as expected, late.

The agenda item was: *Local Service Improvement*. It was innocuous sounding, yet Lexi knew that it would have a deeper implication than most at the meeting would realize. She had a reason to be here that would satisfy her employers or anyone who knew her official secret remit. She was trying to focus on the details of the proposal so that she could counter them in her report.

"Spending on leisure and educational activities was at capacity and we need to find new ways to fund, restructuring, ..." Lexi tuned out. She realized they were winning in their ploy to bore everyone to indifference. It wasn't complicated, they were asking for money to be shifted around which looked like it was going to a better use, in reality, they were going to give less to the Volt, this would eventually make it unsustainable at its current location and then they would swoop in with a buyer ready to offer a good price and a cheaper alternative location already available. They were two steps ahead. Who did they have on the committee that was being used—or maybe paid—to bring this forward? No one was paying attention. The local newspaper had gone home, and Nathan didn't have any power to block it. Residents could have a say, but only the council members could vote. There was little opposition. The motion passed unanimously.

16

Patrice had cleaned the house from top to bottom. She needed to wait until Frank got home before she finished making dinner. She cracked the eggs that she would slow bake in a spicy sauce. If she wasn't careful, they would come out too hard. He got annoyed when that happened even though it was usually because she had to leave them warming while he sat in his office. As she looked at the discarded shells, she remembered an article she'd read in a magazine at the hair salon, "walking on eggshells," that's how the woman described her life with her emotionally abusive husband. At first, he was charming and generous, yet as time passed, he watched her every move and controlled every aspect of her life. That wasn't anything like their relationship, she tried to convince herself. Frank only got irritated with her because of how tired he was.

She needed an evening free from arguments. Frank wasn't violent, yet he could be mean. Their arguments had become more aggressive and frequent, and she had to keep reminding herself that at least he didn't hit her. It didn't seem like a thought she should have in a happy marriage. He rarely apologized. He might pour her a drink or run her a bath, yet often ruined it and made it feel that what had happened was her fault. Recently, she didn't even have to do anything to upset him. He was in a permanent state of irritation. He claimed to have a lot on his mind, yet he refused to discuss any of it with her. She didn't know where he was half the time.

He'd taken the advice of a guy on a daytime TV show. According to the relationship expert, she shouldn't bother him for at least thirty minutes when he got in from work. Taking relationship advice from a celebrity seemed suspect, yet even saying that had caused an argument.

"Wasn't it you who said I should embrace my softer side?" he hissed. "Let's try couples' counseling," he mimicked her voice. "Well, that's all they are going to tell you, the same stuff the guy on the TV says."

She'd only mentioned counseling because they'd had a rough patch early, she thought it would strengthen their relationship and avoid any future problems. She'd been idealistic, believing their romance was almost perfect, and wanted to keep it that way. Today, she needed some human connection. She realized too late she'd made a big mistake tackling him the moment he walked in the door. "How was your day? I hope you're hungry I'm making the egg dish you like."

He looked at her with disgust, "You could have tidied yourself up a bit."

She realized her hair was still tied up messily on top of her head and she was wearing a stained apron to protect the new dress he'd bought for her underneath.

"I give you this beautiful home and a life most women would die for, and you still complain. All I ask is that you take a bit of care of yourself, and you can't even do that."

His bad temper was almost bearable, yet his constant sniping about her looks was wearing her down. She fought off the thought that him picking out her clothes was controlling. At first, he brought her things that were beautiful and expensive. She couldn't possibly have objected to that. Later, the items became less to her taste, items she imagined he'd seen other women wear. She had difficulty squeezing into them, and his face would display a mixture of disappointment and disgust. His latest gift made her furious. The presentation of a fancy gift box seemed to offer the promise of silk and lacy lingerie, yet among the tissue she found only industrial strength "shape-wear." She had wanted to throw it back in his face, yet after she tried it on under her favorite dress, she had to admit it made her look slender. It was hard to stay mad at him when the item miraculously hid her excess weight. It made her realize it was only a small amount she needed to lose. Why was it so hard? Frank made a point of telling her that this was a temporary and emergency measure, and he didn't expect her to need it come the New Year Ball.

Frank poured himself a stiff drink and escaped into the study. Today, she needed to talk to him. It wasn't even a big deal. She just wanted to sound him out about an ad she'd seen for a weekend retreat. Maybe Lexi or some of the others might want to go. It felt safer to wait to ask them until she got the okay from Frank. A weekend just for her and friends, to do fun stuff, it had been so long since she'd spent time with anyone else but Frank. She'd never asked for anything like this of him before. She couldn't see why it would be a problem, yet Patrice couldn't pretend that the emotion she was feeling wasn't a lot like fear.

Her first mistake was to ask to speak to him before the allotted thirty minutes. She knocked on the door and entered. He was talking to someone, a woman, on a video call. The voice sounded familiar. Maybe she should have waited, not come straight in, though why the hell shouldn't she? She wasn't a child; it was her house too. His instinct to close the laptop as he noticed her was probably a mistake on his part. It made him look guilty, yet he was the one who was angry.

He steered her away from his study and into the kitchen. "What the hell is so important that you cannot give me half an hour? Do you know how hard I work? I still have some loose ends to tie up when I get home. I don't know what is wrong with you lately, but you're becoming a pain in my ass."

Patrice was shocked and felt tears coming into her eyes. When she felt that mixture of anger and hurt, he always made her want to cry and it made her angry because she didn't want to be weak. She had done nothing wrong, but he was treating her like some underling, like she worked for him, and she was in trouble. She realized that bringing up the weekend now would be a disaster. She couldn't figure out how to defuse the situation. It was as if there was steam coming from his ears he was so angry. What had got into him? He normally kept it under control.

She felt like something was shifting, other thoughts she'd pushed to the back of her mind were coming to her. The group had been talking about a TV show they'd all seen. A woman was being manipulated by her boyfriend. She was the only one who couldn't see it. Patrice had grown quiet as they discussed the plot. She had become horrified as she realized she could have written that script. She'd brushed it off, but now it came back like a smack in the face. If Frank was guilty of the same behavior, she would stop it here and now, she wouldn't be like those weak women, she would stand up to him. She knew he loved her, but maybe she'd allowed him to get away with too much and now it was time to stop.

"Frank, there's no need to be like this. I just wanted to talk about an opportunity I had to go away for a weekend with the running group. There's a retreat coming up. I thought it would be good for you to have some time on your own, and I could have a little break. I just wanted to make sure you were okay with it and confirm the dates before I committed to anything." She couldn't admit the weekend was her idea, it might make him angrier. She should have stopped there, yet she felt reckless as she added. "Whatever you were doing in there that is so secretive, maybe you should tell me what that's all about instead of taking it out on me."

Frank stepped forward, and it forced her to move back against the wall. For a brief second, she thought he was going to hit her. His face had changed again. It was red; he clenched his teeth, and she saw his balled fists. He stepped back and leaned against the kitchen counter with his arms folded, calmer yet somehow more aggressive.

"The group, oh you mean your little running friends, that group? They're going to take you away with them for a fun weekend. Maybe it's time you learned some facts. They are not your friends, they're not your group. They are an investment. I paid for them to be your friends."

Patrice would've argued that this was ludicrous if it wasn't such a strange thing to say. What did he mean he paid for them? Of course, they were her friends.

"I didn't pay all of them," he amended. "Lucky for me they came as a package, but the dumb, loud one has been on my payroll for months. I hired her to be your friend when you didn't have any. I had to get that fat off you. She was happy to take my money she's probably laughing behind your back. Probably told the rest of them and they'll be laughing too. You don't have any real friends, all the ones you have are because I made it happen."

Any resolve Patrice had evaporated. She broke down into sobs. Only her husband could do this to her. Ruin the one thing that mattered: the group who she trusted and liked. Could this be true, that they all knew? But why would the others be a part of it? It made little sense. "So that's who I am? A rich bitch who lives on the hill in the gated community, who needs her husband to buy her friends."

Frank saw he'd overplayed his hand. "Sweetheart, I was trying to help. You were miserable, and you needed to find some friends, so I just asked around for someone who would help you get to know some new people. I hired Deb because she was into running. I thought you'd tire of her and ditch her after a few months, when you felt comfortable and didn't need her anymore. Unfortunately, she is like a parasite. She is blackmailing me. If I didn't keep paying her, she would tell you and make it seem worse than it really was. That's who I was talking to on the computer when you came in. That's why I was so angry. It scared me you would find out. I did it for you. I wanted to make you happy."

Patrice had not felt so thoroughly miserable for as long as she could remember. She felt powerless. Who could she talk to if they all knew? She was lost. They were often talking quietly in corners. They had meetings and didn't invite her. Surely, they wouldn't be having meetings just to talk about her. She didn't know what to do. She wanted to confront Deb. The more she thought about it, the more she realized how weird Deb been with her after the first couple of months. That was probably when she started blackmailing her husband. What the hell else had she been doing?

Patrice was going to sort this out, and she was going to find out what everybody else knew. She knew she didn't want to lose the group. She hoped that this wasn't true, even though she couldn't see why Frank would have admitted his part. Once again, he was all she had. Who else could she talk to about this?

She realized that if there was one straight shooter, it was Lexi.

17

———

Lᴇxɪ ᴛʀɪᴇᴅ to keep the group on track. They didn't seem to realize that they needed to follow the training schedule if they wanted to complete the race coming up. "Has anyone heard from Patrice? She's already missed one run. She can't afford to miss another."

They'd all signed up for the 10K including Nathan and Amanda. It gave them a legitimate reason to hang out together. Nathan was stretching and didn't look in a hurry. "Maybe give her a few more minutes, it's still early."

Deb looked like she might know something, but Lexi knew this was not the time to get into it. Patrice arrived as they were about to start the run. She didn't seem to be in the mood for talking and put in earbuds, breaking one of the group's unwritten rules. They ran most of the four miles in silence.

When they arrived back at the parking lot, Patrice pulled out her earbuds and stood for a moment, staring at Deb. "How much is the going rate for a friend in this town? Did you come as a group package, or did he pay you separately? Oh no, he didn't pay all of you did he? Just you Deb."

Deb stepped back in shock.

Lexi jumped in. "I only found out this week. No one else was involved, let's go inside and get some coffee and talk properly. It's not what you think."

"You—you knew? I thought I could trust you." She turned back to Deb. "And you, you bitch, blackmailing my husband."

Patrice lunged forward. Deb held up her hands. "Oh, hell no, that is not how he is spinning this. Yes he paid me at first, but then he was making me spy on you. I tried to stop. He wouldn't let me. He kept threatening to make it bad for me, well I guess he's done that now."

Amanda and Nathan retreated to the safety of Tea and Two.

Lexi tried again. "Come inside Patrice, I promise you Deb is telling the truth I only found out by accident, and she's been trying to find a way to tell you."

Patrice's face was a picture of misery. For a minute, it seemed she might come inside with them. Then she turned and headed back to her car. She turned on the ignition and laid her head on the steering wheel. Even from a distance they could see she was convulsed in painful lonely sobs. The rest of them convened over coffee. Lexi wanted to follow Patrice, she hated to see how much she was hurting, but didn't know how to reach her and struggled with the unfamiliar emotional territory. She updated the group on what they'd witnessed. Zander joined them and was the only one who was completely out of the loop regarding the revelation about Deb working for Frank.

Deb frowned, then spoke in a flat emotionless voice. "I worried he would tell her. I was on a video call with him when I saw Patrice come into the room. It was a split second, and I wasn't sure if she saw me. When she missed the run, I guessed that something was going on, but I didn't know what to do."

Nathan addressed the group. "I know I keep saying this, but Frank is more dangerous than you all think. It's time to bring

Deb up to speed. He's a weasel, Deb. We've discovered that there's a plot to close the Volt, the plan is break it up and eventually sell it off. Frank is among other things a property developer, we know he's somehow involved. We've been meeting and working together to share what we know and figure out how to stop him."

Deb's head was spinning, "So while I've been trying to get myself out from under Frank's clutches, you've been doing what an undercover investigation?"

Nathan said. "I've been using my sources to find out what he's up to."

Lexi spoke directly to Deb. "You need to find a way to make this right with Patrice and it won't be easy. Frank is clever and for whatever reason he's told her about you, it's going to put us all in jeopardy. You said he's already asking questions. He cannot know that we have been looking into his business. Someone find me some paper."

Zander brought a notepad from behind the counter. They normally groaned when she did this. Lexi could not think without writing her thoughts. Bullet points, circles, and arrows were the way her brain worked. She had to create a map so that she could clear her mind.

Lexi looked directly at Deb. "Frank hired you to run with and encourage Patrice. In his mind, he did it for good intentions, or that's what she thinks now. Deb, that's what he told you, right? At first he made you believe that this was just a way to ease her loneliness."

"Yes, he was cool at first, and I thought it was sweet in a creepy way. He only got weird later when she got closer to us and wanted to hang out more. It seemed like he got jealous."

Lexi was now stabbing the paper with the end of the pen.

"So you have to convince her you were not part of the manipulation without throwing the blame back on Frank."

"But he's told her I'm blackmailing him, which is a lie." Deb looked scared.

Lexi screwed up the paper and tossed it in the trash. She was exasperated, everything seemed to be out of her control. They barely had a plan to save the Volt and the mess between Patrice, Frank and Deb seemed to make it even less likely. "I'm going to deal with this. Everyone just stay out of trouble."

Lexi worried if she didn't do something the situation would get worse. She needed to make a sacrifice and do something she thought she would never do. She headed outside and saw Patrice's unoccupied car.

She sent her a text.

Patrice, there's something I want to tell you. I know you are still around the Volt. Will you meet me?

It was a few minutes before she received a reply, and she didn't have to go far.

I'm by the food trucks.

Lexi walked around the corner and saw Patrice nursing a coffee. It surprised Lexi she'd chosen to stay close by the Volt rather than go home.

She looked coolly at Lexi. "I'm really disappointed in you, that you would cover for her. What is it you've got to tell me? And I want no more excuses. Frank has already told me everything about Deb."

Lexi thought and almost verbalized, "I doubt it." No, she would stick to her plan. She took an envelope from her tote bag and removed a laminated piece of paper. She slid it wordlessly to Patrice, who silently read the newspaper cutting that was yellowed and tattered. Patrice furrowed her brow as she read and was none the wiser as to its relevance as she scanned the article.

Lexi had not presented it in this way for dramatic effect. She simply didn't know how else to begin a conversation like this. The early articles had not named her. They had protected her identity when they thought her mother's death may have been a homicide. Lexi took the clipping from Patrice. She looked at it one more time and spoke with emotion she had never allowed Patrice to see. "'The girl with the body,' that's how I was known for many years."

"That was you?"

"No one here knows. I changed my last name. It was a long time ago and thankfully people have finally forgotten. I've never made friends easily. I, too, was manipulated into joining the group—encouraged, really—not by a partner but by my therapist. I was going to do one race and quit. I would have fulfilled my therapist's social engineering experiment to force me to make friends, prove it had failed and then she wouldn't dump me as she threatened. Until I joined the group, she was one of only two friends. How sad is that?"

Patrice was softening slightly. "I'm so sorry you went through that, I'm sure your life has been hard, but Deb still betrayed me."

Lexi had to decide right now if she was going to push further. "Patrice, I've told you something that I didn't want to tell anyone. I did that because I don't want you to lose the friendships in the group. I know how important they have become to me, and I'm guessing that they are the same for you. As I've already taken a risk and told you about myself, I'm going to ask you a question. Patrice, how much do you trust your husband?" As the word's left her mouth Lexi saw she'd made a mistake, she noticed a slight narrowing of Patrice's lips along with a hardening of her eyes, her anger had returned.

Patrice's next move was unexpected. She took out a small silver filigree case from her purse—it looked like an antique—and flipped it open to reveal a row of slender cigarettes. She lit one and exhaled smoke in Lexi's direction. An act of war.

"So that's how you're gonna play it, make Frank the bad guy so you can feel good about yourselves? He's my husband, he gets things wrong sometimes, but he does his best. Who do you expect me to believe? Deb over him?"

Lexi felt she may as well keep going, she had nothing to lose.

"Do you know what he does in his business? I mean you know for sure he secretly hired Deb. Whatever you think of her motives, she claims he asked her to spy on you. I know you don't want to believe that, but deep down, do you completely trust him? Deb's scared of Frank. She's been trying to find a way of telling you but was worried what he might do to her. So, I'll ask you again, how much do you trust Frank? And Patrice, what is it with the smoking?"

"I've been secretly smoking for a few months; it's been a stressful time. I would drink, but Frank always comments on the calories, so I smoke, no calories, see. We all keep secrets in marriages. Frank conducts important business, and he doesn't talk to me about his work. He sometimes works with people who I'm not entirely comfortable with, but I doubt he'd do anything to harm Deb. Why would he lie and say she was blackmailing him?"

Lexi was frustrated, she wasn't getting anywhere and had begun to wish she hadn't shared her past with Patrice.

"Think about it this way, the 5K training program started in February, Deb signed a contract for three months to get you through the race. Frank will have that contract somewhere." Lexi paused to do the calculation in her head. "He's paid her for almost six additional months. Do you really believe he would have done that because he was scared that she would tell you?

Does Frank allow people to extort money from him, or was he the one who insisted she kept working for him, which makes more sense?"

Patrice still looked unconvinced, "So why do you care anyway? what does it matter to you what Frank does in his business?"

Lexi wasn't sure how to move forward. "You know he advertised the job? He interviewed Deb. He even had a lawyer present—Celeste Collins, you mentioned before that you know her. Why would he need a lawyer to keep Deb quiet if he did it in your best interests? Deb didn't know what she was getting into or that she would get to know you and like you, she tried hard to get out of the contract. Under other circumstances, you would've become real friends and maybe you still can."

Patrice sneered at hearing Celeste's name. "Frank gives me a good life and I can only hope it comes from honest labor. I've stayed away from the dinners and charity fundraisers and refused to befriend the fakes, and the likes of Celeste Collins. But Lexi, I'm married to Frank, he might not be perfect, but I'm not going to choose a bunch of people I barely know over him. I'm still not seeing why this is your business. You're not my mother."

Lexi decided it was time to reveal her hand. "I know that's not how you feel, the group and this place it means something to you, like it does for all of us. We're concerned that some areas of the Volt are under threat. Zander is worried about his business, he's probably weeks away from losing Tea and Two for good. Amanda learned the Eden is in jeopardy, and she can't just up and leave to the other side of town with a crop of native plants and a flock of rescued wild animals." Lexi only referenced information that had come from Zander and Amanda, and nothing about the Volt that Lexi might know from her brief. "They're wondering if Frank might have said anything, or if he might be involved. I know you're mad with us but think about what life might be like if there was no Volt, imagine Tribune without this place. Please don't say anything to Frank but if you know anything...."

Patrice interrupted Lexi as she rose from the table. "So not only Deb, but the rest of them are whispering behind my and Frank's back. Sounds like you are all paranoid. I won't say anything to Frank for now, but I think it might be time I started looking for another running group."

Patrice walked back towards her car, stopping to light another cigarette.

Lexi felt wrecked. She craved a drink, or something else to distance her thoughts and feelings. She wanted to be at home. She aimed for the food trucks instead. Takeout would blunt the adrenaline crash.

18

———

Lexi realized her stomach was growling. Her prior trauma sometimes manifested in struggles with eating. Some of the quirkier therapies she underwent at The Sanctuary were helpful, although some she still rolled her eyes at when she thought about them. One theory was that she'd never forgiven herself for "inhaling" molecules from her mother's body as it lay decomposing, or that she'd eaten the tropical fish from the tank when the food ran out. The memory of what really happened to the fish was uncomfortable to disclose. It had surfaced much later in a therapy session. Her loneliness and desperation led her to climb up and scoop out the fish. She'd wanted to play with them and didn't understand they couldn't survive outside the tank. After each one died; she flushed them down the toilet. Her mom had taught her to flush, and that part of the apartment was the only place where she could breathe without the pervading smell. The window was cracked a little allowing just enough air to take a fresh deep breath.

The food trucks would pack up soon. She could have gone inside and bought something from Zander, but she'd done all the talking she could handle for one day. She rarely cooked at the apartment. It made far too much mess. She liked her kitchen to be sparkling. Cleanliness was the one thing that made her happy.

She was about to walk over to order when she realized there was someone behind her. There were often people hanging around. Some regulars from the Harbor had made it their base, and she had no fear of them. Many she knew by name. As she turned, she saw someone she didn't recognize. Nathan had made her paranoid. She imagined if someone was following, it would be a trench-coated investigator or a man in a dark suit. Instead, in front of her was a man, bundled up as if he was in the Arctic in the 70 degree night. His attire made her even more suspicious. She stepped back. Shit, was he armed? Was he going to shoot her? While these thoughts were going through her mind, he put up his arms in a defensive mode.

"I'm sorry I didn't mean to scare you; I just want to talk."

"Who are you? What do you want?"

"Can we go somewhere to talk, it's complicated and I need to tell you something. It would be better if you were sitting down."

"Are you a reporter?"

"No, I promise I'm not, and I mean you no harm."

Lexi had set her mind on a banh mi sandwich and this guy was not going to stop her from placing her order. She pointed in the direction she was heading. "I'm getting food. You can tell me what you have to say in the five minutes it will take them to make my dinner."

They sat on the wooden picnic tables, that were still damp from an earlier shower. The sun was setting, and Lexi could feel its warmth on her back. "I'm going to ask you one more time. Are you a reporter? I'll know if you are lying, and," she looked at her watch, "you have 4 minutes and 30 seconds."

After he reassured her, he began his story. "I've had twenty-eight years to get this speech right. I've written hundreds of versions, in letters and emails that I never sent. We met once when you were a child. I'm deeply sorry and ashamed to tell you I'm the reason your mother died. I'm Matthew West, Dr. Matthew West, the doctor who missed what should have been obvious and sent your mother away to die."

Lexi suddenly felt dizzy, as if the ground had moved beneath her. A wave of nausea swept through her body. She whispered, "You're Doctor Death."

Dr. West breathed heavily and continued. Lexi wanted him to stop. This man, sitting in front of her, here in Tribune, had been at the core of her years of misery, of her loss. She would never know her mother, and it was because of him. She couldn't concentrate on the words, she'd missed the most important part as she was trying to breathe, she needed the whole story, but he was talking about them finding her mom, she wanted his story.

"I read it in the paper, about the kids who found you, they thought you couldn't talk. There were photos. I knew it was you. I remembered your eyes; you were staring into the camera, and I knew, I had caused this."

Lexi had stopped counting the minutes. Her food order had been sitting on the food truck counter for over 10 minutes. She'd forgotten her hunger; her emotions had taken over every sensation in her body.

Dr. West sobbed, "I'm sorry I should have written it down. I wanted to explain, but seeing you here, so alive, I can't..."

Years of the best therapy and every alternative treatment available, couldn't disconnect her from the pain and trauma of her experience. She wanted to talk to him, to ask questions, to know more, but she couldn't physically handle any more right now. She got up and ran. He yelled after her about the hotel he was staying at; she caught half of it as her feet carried her as far away from him as fast as she could. He'd opened a door she had tried to seal shut. She had never dealt with her anger, and now she had someone to direct it towards.

19
___

Lᴇxɪ ʜᴀᴅ sᴘᴇɴᴛ ᴀʟᴍᴏsᴛ forty-eight hours in her apartment. She had paced, practiced deep breathing, eaten her emergency ice-cream supply, she had appetite for little else. She had tried every therapeutic technique to block the thoughts of *him*. The knowledge that *he* was here in Tribune allowed her no peace.

The unexpected appearance of Doctor Death had uncovered her trauma. Sounds, smells, the taste overtook her. She drifted awake, asleep, awake, shivering, so cold? All the windows open, she'd had to get rid of the smell. Her face wet, crying, sobs that hurt, not her tears, little Lexi's, alone afraid. Her mom whispered, what was she saying? "phone" it needed numbers to make it work, she didn't know the numbers. She was hungry, she dreamed of cookies.

Lexi woke fully now, with the details of the unwanted memories, they'd been hidden from her mind for many years. Her unconscious mind did its job, protecting her by suppressing them. Now they surfaced, and she needed to use everything she had to face the details of the days she spent alone with her mother's decaying corpse.

Lexi knew, of course, what had happened to her: she'd read

the headlines; she was the *girl with the body*. She was remembered for the horror. Though she was infamous during her youth, as she grew older, worse atrocities were uncovered, people locked in dungeons, kidnappings and human trafficking. Her tragedy was an accident, there was no evil sadist, just a misdiagnosis and not worthy of further newsprint. For this, she was grateful.

People still sometimes remembered the story, and she hated how once they knew it was her, it was all they wanted to talk about. They remembered the photographs of her looking into the camera with enormous sad eyes, dirty and starving. She had been a pitiful sight when they found her.

Lexi needed help, she needed Lorna.

It was dark now, quiet. She couldn't hear anything not even her mom's breathing, better to sleep, her tummy didn't hurt if she slept, there was no more food.

Lexi woke, how long had she been here? She needed food, to be clean, she needed Lorna. She desperately searched for her phone, this couldn't go on. The therapy was imperfect because Lexi had needed to keep control. Today, she would do whatever it took. She hit the speed dial number and breathed. "Lorna, I need to see you. It's an emergency."

"Lexi, of course. I'm not in the office today, but I can be there in about an hour. Will that work?"

Lexi knew Lorna would know it was serious. Even in her darkest hours, Lexi liked to stick to the schedule. Lorna had an office near her home. It was a small unit just a few doors away. She refused to compromise her privacy by allowing clients into her home. She had once told Lexi that her husband thought the expense was ludicrous when they had a room they could use, but she was adamant. Lexi understood. Lorna did deep emotional work and needed to let go of the connection when she went home. Distance between her professional and personal life was as important to her as her safety.

Lexi was waiting for Lorna when she arrived. A late October day was too cold to be outside with hair wet from the shower, and shoes with no socks, but Lexi couldn't feel anything, even though she shivered. She refused the ginger tea she normally enjoyed during their sessions but accepted the blanket that Lorna offered.

"He's here in Tribune, Doctor Death, the man who killed my mother. He came to find me."

As the story spilled out, Lexi confessed it had happened two days ago, she'd felt unable to talk to anyone, and hid in her apartment. She'd wanted to tell Remi, the only other person who would understand, but knew he had a huge concert that weekend, and she wasn't prepared to ruin it.

Lorna tried to get Lexi to see it from another angle as she had done on many previous occasions.

"Lexi, Dr. West's arrival has tipped your world off its axis. Even after all these years and every technique we've tried, you've resisted looking at parts of what you went through. Your feelings towards Dr. West have always been a roadblock to your healing. Now he's here maybe it's the right time to deal with that."

Lexi was shaking her head. "I don't want his excuses and he's not getting my forgiveness if that's what he's expecting."

"There is a theory, Lexi, that when you've tried everything else, the thing you are avoiding might be the answer. Let's talk a little about what we know. Dr. Matthew West is not Doctor Death, as you have sometimes referred to him, so let's stop that. He didn't kill your mother, he was a young inexperienced and overwhelmed doctor, working the graveyard shift in an underfunded hospital. He misdiagnosed your mother. It's possible that she might have been treated successfully if it had been properly diagnosed but the nature of sepsis means it's often missed, and this tragedy is not uncommon. You don't blame your aunt, or the nurse, you have been fixated on this man for years. Maybe it's time to let it go."

Lexi was unmoved. "My mom took days to die, and I was alone with her while she rotted. He should have listened to her."

Lorna paused. "I know this has been a terrible shock, but you are fighting a battle that is unnecessary. How does it help you to keep holding onto this anger? It is an unproductive emotion that is poisoning your capacity for a happy life. Even if he hadn't come back, it would always have been there, eating away at you.

"I have a suggestion you are not going to like. If you want to deal with this pain, you need to talk to the man who you have decided is a monster, and shatter the power you've given this imaginary version of him. He is a man with flaws, and he came back to look for you. He didn't have to. Why not contact him? See what you can discover that will give you the peace you are looking for. We could do it here where you feel safe and I can facilitate, with his consent, of course. He's come this far to find you. I doubt he will refuse."

Lexi whispered. "No thanks. If I ignore him, he'll go back to wherever he came from."

20

———

SHE WANTED to be angry with Lorna, yet as Lexi reflected, she knew she was being unfair. Lorna had always been flexible, allowed Lexi to do what was comfortable and only pushed her when she felt it was necessary. The truth was, Lexi hadn't fully engaged in the therapeutic process. She had grown to like Lorna and felt she was disappointing her by admitting that she was still a mess psychologically. Some people clean their house before the housekeeper arrived. Lexi mentally cleaned up her act and painted on the quirky, almost-happy face when she was often screaming inside.

She kept many of her anxieties hidden, refusing to believe them to be a problem. Lexi's life trajectory resulted from something that shouldn't have happened; someone didn't take a concern seriously, and it ended in tragedy. If an anxiety was worrying about things that never happened, she didn't have anxiety she reasoned. Lexi worried about things that did, could, and had happened. She avoided the potential for risk, pain, and danger whenever possible. What others considered rituals, to her were risk aversion strategies.

On an occasion where she opened up to Lorna, it almost

destroyed their professional relationship. Lexi had studied micro-expressions and was a master at observing people's faces. She could detect a slight shift that would be imperceptible to anyone else. Others might have said she was looking for it, but she knew without a doubt that she had seen it. "A baby monitor?" Lorna's face was calm, yet a slight quiver of her mouth betrayed her normally benign demeanor. Lexi saw what? Not mockery that was too strong, but there was something, a flicker of ridicule, was Lorna laughing at her?

"Yes, would it work in a coffin?"

Lexi had never before vocalized her fear of being buried alive. She knew to some it seemed ridiculous, but it was one of her night terrors. If she could have a prevention strategy, she would at least stop thinking about it. Obtrusive thoughts were a common theme, yet this one had at its core something she could solve. She wanted to explore the option of having a communication device in her coffin with her, for it to be monitored for a period after her burial to be sure there was no sign of life and she wanted Lorna to help her put this in place legally as part of her will.

Lorna would later say that she was genuinely curious rather than dismissive or unprofessional. She was used to Lexi coming out with unusual ideas, yet always had respected her and understood how her background had shaped her fears. For Lexi, that quirk of the mouth was a betrayal. She left the session abruptly and said she would find someone else to help her. Lexi was not normally overly dramatic. She later learned that Lorna had been deeply concerned about her reaction. Thankfully Lorna was invested in helping Lexi. She sent a selection of Lexi's favorite chocolates along with a note, she was there to continue their work whenever Lexi was ready.

When an intrusive thought started, nothing would stop it, it had to run its course. It grew until Lexi could barely breathe. It then looped back, and all the details would play out again. The worst thing that could happen to her became like a movie on repeat. She would counter it with all the reasons the terror wouldn't happen, but her reality was never strong enough to defeat it. Usually it lasted for a few hours, but sometimes when there was the tiniest element of possibility in the thought, she would have to wait until she could find evidence to the contrary.

If she felt a bump in the road on her rare drives, she would check the newspapers the next day for a story about a hit and run, cooking for others would never happen as she worried she would poison her guests, or they had an unknown peanut allergy that would cause literal death by chocolate pudding. Some of her obsessive thoughts were not uncommon. Losing her car in a parking lot, getting lost, locking herself out. But some were much deeper, and she struggled to say them out loud.

The rituals came out of nowhere. It was as if a voice told her to do them, her own inner thoughts. What harm could come from walking the long way around the kitchen before leaving the house or wearing a particular pair of socks? Every time she told herself that a ritual was stupid, she would counter it with another thought, what harm could it do and what if she didn't do it and then something bad happened?

It was two days since the session with Lorna and four since the arrival of the doctor. She'd thought of nothing else. She'd managed a run with the group the day after the session with Lorna. Patrice had not shown up. It gave them the opportunity to share updates on the Volt—there was little new to report. Lexi was grateful no one was focused on her. She needed to take back control of her life before it was too late.

She asked Nathan to meet her at Tea and Two around noon. She had work to do, her deadline was looming, but couldn't focus. She needed to get out of her head and decide what to do next. She chose the furthest, most private booth and tried not to look over at Zander while Nathan ordered her a double espresso at her request.

She took a sip of her coffee before asking. "Nathan, do you know who I am?"

Nathan didn't need her to explain the question. "I wasn't prying, I background check everyone who comes into my close circle. Not everyone is who they seem. I have to be careful. Believe it or not people also want to know who I am."

Lexi smiled and whispered, "I'm the *Girl with the Body* and you're *The Fly Guy*."

Nathan looked mock offended. "Me? By the way, there's no "The" I understand. It's just Fly Guy. And seeing as you asked first, do you know about my background?"

Lexi shook her head and felt a little ashamed that she'd never asked about his family.

"I'm from here, my family are. My story is not as tragic as yours, but it has shaped who I am. Being gay in this area has not always been easy. My family wouldn't accept that I wasn't just in their words 'going through a phase.' They forced me to go to conversion therapy, when that didn't work, they tried other methods."

Lexi was wide eyed; she saw the pain in Nathan's face. "Are you still in touch with them?"

"They're still here, but I don't see them. I divorced them." Nathan used air quotes to emphasize divorced. "I no longer consider them my parents. I threatened to sue them for what they put me through. I was screwed up for a long time. They gave me a considerable sum of money to go away and not bring any more shame on the family. My divorce settlement, I guess."

Lexi was stunned. "They know what year this is right?"

"Let's not talk about them anymore, it depresses me. What do you need? I know you aren't yourself."

"Can you find someone for me." She had written his name on a sticky note.

Nathan said, "I need a little more than a name."

"He's staying in one of the local hotels. He arrived last week. He's the doctor who was responsible for my mom's death. He came looking for me, but I don't know much more than that. I can describe him to you."

"I didn't think there was any evidence of negligence or foul play in your mom's death. What do you want me to do when I find him? I'm not the breaking people's legs type."

Lexi knew Nathan was trying to lighten the mood, but she wasn't ready for jokes. "I need to know if he's staying and for how long. I guess I need to hear him out before he goes."

"He shouldn't be too hard to find." Nathan said, "I have a question. Why Tribune? It's so close to where it all happened. What are you doing here? Presumably you could work anywhere."

"Well, I could ask you the same question. Maybe it's my destiny, to meet the person who caused it and finally put it to rest. Though I'm still not sure I'm ready."

"I'll see if I can find him. Let's meet here later."

"Thanks Nathan, I appreciate it. Tell me, how do you know so much about the people in this town? I know you won't tell me if you really are a hacker, but you seem to be able to find information that I can't."

Nathan smiled. "I get to know people; I listen and learn who I can trust. People who are too scared to do anything with information they have bring it to me and, if possible, I expose it. My persona of a not very smart guy with a political beef doesn't fit with the articulate writer behind the articles that oust corrupt politicians. The information started as a trickle and now I can't stop it. A lot of this stuff I don't want to know. I feel like the thrift store that gets mounds of trash bags left outside when they are closed, it's not all usable. People's romantic affairs for example, are none of my business, unless they're doing it on council time and using their expense account."

Lexi raised an eyebrow. "Do you know anything like that about Frank, personal, sleazy stuff?"

"Maybe. It hasn't been relevant until recently, though it's important not to get bogged down with local scandal. So long as it's legal, I'm not the morality police."

Lexi looked disappointed at his response. "Patrice deserves to be happy and not to be controlled by him. Maybe if you find anything concrete, you'll let me know."

It surprised Lexi when she received a text within an hour. "Got him. No need for the thumbscrews."

While waiting for Nathan at Tea, she tried to focus on something else. The sweet flaky pastry with cream and fruit filling would normally have disappeared in a few bites. Today it sat untouched. The mere thought of this guy was enough to put her off her food. Zander had tried to engage her in conversation. She felt bad but knew she would have told him everything if she began talking. As far as she knew, he didn't know her past yet. It was all going to come out. It seemed out of her control.

Nathan swooped in and pointed at the pastry she had now pushed away. He ate it before she could open her mouth. "Dr. Matthew West, as we guessed, didn't give up so easily. He's staying at the little B&B. Poor fella he was probably more comfortable in a tent in Africa—that's where he's come from by the way. He goes by Matthew, and he is a broken mess. He will meet you wherever, whenever, you are his only reason for being here. I felt sorry for the guy."

"What did he say? What happened?"

Nathan was enjoying himself. "I was a badass. I played the role perfectly."

"You weren't supposed to be playing a role, you were just supposed to find him."

Nathan laughed, he could be inappropriately chirpy. "I know, but I wanted to check him out before I put you in a room with him."

"Spill it!"

"Let me set the scene. After I told him I know you, he lets me in. I grab the Do Not Disturb sign and I keep eye contact with him while I hang it on the outside of the door, like in a gangster movie. I close it behind me and then I say, 'She's still figuring out it if she can bear to talk to you and it isn't because she wants to forgive you. She wants answers. I'm here because I want you to know if you make things worse for her, I'll come after you.'"

Lexi groaned. "I still don't know if I want to see him. What did he say?"

"He said he hadn't forgiven himself so doubted you could, and he was here to do anything he could to make amends. He asked if I had any ideas of how he could help you. And I want to talk to you about that, I do have an idea. I have his phone number. What do you want to do next?"

Lexi thought for a minute. "I need this to be over, but I can't deal with the details. Here's Lorna, my therapist's number. Can you and she figure out the arrangements? And make it soon before I change my mind."

21

———

As she entered the consulting room from the waiting area, Lexi wondered where she would sit. Lorna had pre-empted this concern. She'd pushed back her couch and replaced it with two chairs, even though the couch was rarely used for laying on. Lexi would be more comfortable sitting a distance away rather than sharing an intimate space with Doctor Death.

She worried that an overwhelming emotional response that she couldn't control would overtake her rational side. She'd cut Dr. West off before he could tell his full story. She wanted to know it all today; she wanted to have all the gaps in her mother's life filled in, even though she knew he would have little to add. Sometimes when she thought of her mother, when she had separated the dead mom from the real one, she got flashes of emotion that were good. Her face was young, her skin smelled of roses, and she held Lexi tightly. Twenty-eight years later and the feeling of grief could still come and surprise her with a powerful intensity, as if her loss was new.

Lorna had asked Lexi to come early so they could have a session. Whatever Lorna did, Lexi knew it would be unorthodox. There would be a Lorna twist, a WTF moment. It better not include screaming. Once had been enough, and she also wasn't prepared to go back in the womb or do past life regression. She wanted a referee. Even though this wasn't even her idea, she realized that she craved it, but only to hear what Dr. West had to say.

"He's coming here of his own free will Lexi. If this meeting is to be of any use, it needs to be done appropriately. Scaring him off will help no one. We need some ground rules. Let's decide what you are prepared to tell him, what is off the table, and when this session is over I encourage you to consider doing some work together. Allow him to talk, to tell his story. It sounds like he has been wanting to tell you for a long time."

Lexi paused and then said. "This is my session. I'm not ready to even think about forgiveness. And before I hear his story, I have something I want to say."

Lorna realized there was nothing else to say.

Dr. West arrived. He asked them to call him Matthew.

Lorna laid out the ground rules. "Lexi has something she wants to say before we begin."

Lexi looked at him. She wanted him to be a monster so she could hate him, but she saw the man he might have been if their paths hadn't crossed. His face told more of his story than his words ever could, yet she couldn't allow herself to have sympathy for him right now. She was fighting with her physiology, she had harnessed her emotions but her body had other ideas. Waves of nausea and a feeling of light-headedness threatened to overtake her.

"The cab driver who took my mom to the hospital was on record as saying she looked very sick. You sent her home with a couple of pain pills. She died a miserable and painful death, and I was left with her body for days. What can you add to that story that could make me feel any better?"

Matthew held tightly onto his water glass and began. "I'm

not here to try to justify myself. I was a new doctor and was finally getting over my fear of making mistakes. Most of the people who came into the ER on a Saturday night were drunk or hypochondriacs. I wasn't getting enough sleep. I thought if I took something, just a pick-me-up, it would be alright, just a few more weeks of taking what I needed from the pharmacy.

"The day your mother came in I had taken extra of everything. The neighbor's dog had been barking half the night and even the sleeping pills hadn't been able to blot out the noise. By the time I got to work I was edgy, exhausted and ready to usher any time-wasters out of the door.

"Your mother seemed drugged up herself. I didn't take in any of that information that the triage nurse had recorded about the scratch on her arm. I didn't even give her a tetanus shot. They didn't officially blame me for her death, but as soon as I learned what had happened, I resigned. I couldn't bear to do the job anymore. It was like I had been in a trance that I'd finally woken from."

Lexi had been trying her hardest to listen without interrupting, but she needed to know.

"But other people do it every day. Why were you different? Why did you need drugs to do your job?"

Matthew faltered, he looked around the room avoiding Lexi's eyes. "Arrogance maybe or fear. I wasn't prepared to ask for help. No one wants to admit after years of study that they can't hack it."

"So you quit and then what?"

"I did what shamed people with a conscience do. I went off to do charity work. The lives I'd ruined devastated me. Though there was no way of knowing if your mother would have survived, I knew I was guilty of not caring enough, of being reckless and for leaving a child—you—without a mother and likely with trauma that would be with you for the rest of your life.

"The chance to do charity work in Kenya dropped into my lap. Much of what was needed didn't require a doctor. When I arrived, I did anything they asked, sometimes holding a flashlight to illuminate makeshift clinics for emergency surgeries conducted in the dark, in fields, in huts, in alleyways. Sight restored by cataract operations done in conditions that would horrify coworkers back home. There was no paperwork, no cover your ass disclaimers, there was just the work, doing the best you could with what you had. I went initially for a year."

"But you stayed far longer than that," Lexi confirmed coolly.

"I found a purpose. The clinic I work at doesn't need me like they once did. I knew it was time to find you."

Lexi shifted in her chair and then stood; her tone had changed as if her rage had been simmering. "Well, I'm glad that you've had such fun in Camp Africa, but tell me, before you left, how quickly did you realize that the dead woman on the news was my mother?"

"Immediately. Even though I'd seen hundreds of patients, when they showed your photograph, I recognized you. I was horrified that my negligence caused your mother to suffer."

"Caused her to die, you mean." Lexi was losing patience, she sat again.

"I knew, yes, I knew. I am so very sorry."

Lexi was struggling to feel any empathy for him. Her emotions were too raw, as if she had just lost her mother yesterday.

"I thought of you all the time and wondered what I could do to make reparation. One day I would show that I was truly sorry."

"How did you find me?"

"I searched online for a while and saw occasional news

items until you dropped off the news cycle. I learned you'd been at The Sanctuary, but they wouldn't tell me anything. I kept looking and worked out when you would graduate, thought I would find a school photo, a name maybe. But of course, you graduated early. I finally saw an article about the *Girl with the Body* being top of the graduating class."

"I kept my past under wraps for a long time," Lexi said "Then I found a friend who I trusted, and foolishly shared my story with. She turned out to be just another user who saw a way to make a few bucks. So, you found me. You see someone who looks like they are doing okay, top of my college class. But years of living in an institution and every possible type of therapy have not been able to fix me. When I wake up in the night in terror, I'm still the girl with the body, who wonders if anyone will save her. I don't know why you came back, or what you want to achieve. I can't give you absolution." Lexi addressed her next comment to Lorna. "I think we're done; dredging everything up is not helping."

Matthew's mouth trembled as he struggled to speak. "I don't know what else I can say or do, I'm so sorry. My intention was not to make you feel worse, I know I can never make up for what I did."

Lexi looked at her nails for a moment, when she looked up at him, she spoke without emotion. "You said you wanted to make amends. How far would you be prepared to go?"

Lorna jumped in. "These sessions are confidential. However, I cannot condone anything unethical. I'm not implying that is what you are suggesting."

"I can't think of anything you could ask that I would have a problem with as long as it was legal and caused no harm."

Lorna reiterated her point. "Lexi, Matthew came here today in order for you to have an honest conversation in a space that was safe and supportive for both of you. Let me be clear

Matthew: You are under no obligation to do anything for Lexi, especially anything which might make you uncomfortable. Lexi, are we clear on this?"

Lexi nodded and readied herself to leave.

Matthew stood, then hesitated as if he wasn't sure if there was anything left to say.

"Nathan will be in touch." Lexi said.

Lorna thanked him for coming and led him out of her office.

Lexi called Nathan on the walk home. "It's over and I'm not sure if it did any good, but whatever you want him for, he'll do it."

22

Lexi didn't go into people's homes often. She politely refused invitations that might have her stuck in a physically uncomfortable position. Other than Deb's, she'd avoided setting foot in anyone else's personal space. When Nathan suggested they meet at his home so he could share his plan without fear of being overheard, she realized she needed to step out of her comfort zone.

He lived in what looked to be a modest single story family home. Once Lexi got through the front door, everything changed. The first thing she noticed was that it wasn't overlooked by anyone, and his security system was excessive for a normal home. There were bolts on the inside of the doors. Was he a Prepper? One of those waiting for the Zombie apocalypse? The windows looked into a normal house, yet they were only really showing a few feet in. Everything inside and beyond that viewed by the windows was invisible, he had created a central area, presumably he had removed interior walls, it left one enormous area with an office and a wall of computer screens, some viewing the outside via security cameras. Lexi was no architect, but she wondered if the removal of the walls has made the building unsafe. That question could wait for later, but first …

"What the hell is this place? Do you live here? Do you own it? What are you doing here?"

"Let's just say sometimes the work I do means I like to know I'm safe in my home."

"And you need all this security. Should I be worried now I'm associating with you?"

"Right now, you aren't of interest or a threat to anyone, and I want to keep it that way." Nathan led her into an area with a small kitchen. "Let's talk about what we know. I don't need to know what you are doing for your assignment. I likely know more than you about what's going on."

Lexi looked relieved. "I don't know what I'm doing anymore. This was simpler before I knew Frank was involved."

"Let's lay it out. We need to know what the plan is for the Volt building. Who's buying it? Who is brokering the deal, what they are planning on doing with it and how far they've got. The council has already cleared the way for a change of use. There's nothing legally to stop them, they just have to prove that they have provided adequate alternative services."

Lexi asked. "My first guess is luxury condos, it's a prime real estate location once they've gentrified the area and got rid of anyone they consider undesirable."

"I thought that too until something came across my radar-- and don't be mad because I've already set something up. I may as well wait and share the news with both of you at the same time." Nathan walked back to the main room, where he saw Matthew standing on the doorstep. "Perfect timing. Sorry Lexi, but after we talked, I realized we don't have a lot of time. I had to speed this along."

Nathan brought Matthew through to the kitchen area

where they all sat. "You both have a lot of questions, so let me tell you as much as I can to save us all time."

Matthew and Lexi looked at each other with resignation.

"Matthew, I've filled you in on the basics. You know the Volt is in jeopardy. I've learned about an investment opportunity for a major real estate development that I think is for the land that the Volt sits on. It's very hush-hush and the only way we can find out more details is for someone to pose as an investor. You are about to have a crash course in acting for the role of your life."

Matthew attempted to stand up, and Nathan put his hand on his shoulder to push him back into his seat. "I don't have any money to be an investor I don't know the first thing about investing." Nathan reassured him, "You don't need any money, you just need to convince them you do."

Lexi put a finger up. "Can't you do this without me?"

Nathan smiled at Lexi, "I think it's only fair you know what I'm proposing. You'll want to know what he discovers."

"Matthew, it's most important to get you in the room to find out what the project is. They will swear you to secrecy, you'll be playing a role, no one knows who you are. They give invites to several people who they believe have the funds to buy in, but this is the first round of funding, they have to tell you what the project is and it will give us a little heads up so we can see what we can do to stop it."

Lexi directed her next question to Nathan but was also looking at Matthew. "I don't mean to be rude, but how do we get a grizzled doctor whose been living in a Kenyan village for decades to look like someone who has a few million to invest? If he screws this up, it will probably come back to me. I'm the only link to him."

"I don't think anyone else is aware of a connection between you both. Matthew, I have to make it look like you have money, and to hope you've not already drawn attention to yourself in town. I have a fixer who's already got you a seat at the table." He led them both to a different room. "We need to find you a suit that looks right. The conundrum is that rich people now wear jeans and t-shirts and wannabes wear suits. Though we're in the South and therefore in another century, so we will go with a suit."

"Who exactly is he meeting with?" Lexi asked.

Nathan was pulling clothes from plastic wrappers and examining them. "I haven't figured that out yet. There are investment groups that bring people together. They might not be the ones doing the deal. Oh, and..." he paused as he held up a sand-colored suit against Matt's chest. "Resort casual? Maybe not. We're going to have to get you a better hotel. Remind me to arrange for a room at the Grand when we're finished here. And no, don't worry, you don't need to pay. You're also going to need a plausible cover story. We are going to create a version of you they will want to talk to."

Lexi didn't want to speak to Matthew but needed to. "Be honest, do you think you can pull it off?"

"I've dealt with danger in Kenya, I've risked the wrath of local gangs. I'm not sure what some local suits in this small town can really do to me. Serving unsweetened tea is the biggest crime I've seen so far. Lexi, I know this means I can't be seen with you, but I hope at some point we can talk some more."

Lexi was not ready to commit to anything. "We'll see."

Nathan agreed. "You need to stay away from each other for now, and please be careful. It would be foolish to underestimate the possibility of bigger players being involved, or even the risks of dealing with small town gangsters. Just stick to the cover story I give you and you should be fine."

Lexi wasn't sure how she felt about the plan. She had an uncharacteristic feeling. It was as if she wanted Matthew to be scared. She was conflicted. Did she want to put him in danger? Lexi struggled to untangle her own feelings.

Matthew went off to try on the clothes Nathan had picked. He looked different in a beautiful suit that fit him reasonably well, though he was a little larger than Nathan.

Lexi asked, "Do you have any shirts? That one is a little tight, the tie almost covers it, but it could give them pause."

Matthew looked down at the slightly gaping buttons. "I don't visit the US often, but when I do, I always bring dress clothes in case I have to attend a funeral."

Nathan handed him a box. "This should make you a little more plausible."

Inside was a tie pin, cufflinks, and a beautiful watch. Matthew raised his eyebrows. "Wow, these are the real deal, aren't they? They would pay for a year's food bill at the hospital. Is this really necessary? I'm now worried about getting mugged."

Nathan insisted. "Some of the local business people who will be at the meeting will not have the means to invest, but they'll look like they do. Style over substance is the name of their game. They will believe you are from out of state. You've lost your accent, which is good. They won't connect you as anyone they should know about. You must look like you are interested and able to buy into whatever scheme is in the works."

23

———————

Lᴇxɪ ɴᴇᴇᴅᴇᴅ to make progress on her report. She'd spent the rest of the weekend in her apartment, reading, researching and creating arguments for and against closing the Volt. She would feed anything she found in favor to Nathan and Amanda to add to their work. She didn't know exactly what they were doing, she just had to trust they were doing something.

Matthew had only a few days to go over the notes that Nathan had provided and Lexi worried that it wasn't enough. She hoped that he wouldn't screw it up. Nathan had said it was a fact-finding mission he just needed to listen and learn.

Lexi had resisted making a follow up appointment with Lorna. She wasn't ready to go over any of her feelings about the meeting with Matthew. The deeper reason though, was her shame, she knew Lorna would see it. Lexi knew she should care that she was putting this man—who she barely knew—into a dangerous situation. She didn't seem to have the capacity to feel concern or pity for him, even when she'd seen that he was genuinely distraught. She felt hard and cruel. She put her focus on her work until the investment meeting was due to happen, then she met with Nathan.

They decided it was safe enough to meet at Tea and Two. Monday evenings at the Volt were quiet, and they would be unlikely to bump into anyone. Besides, Lexi needed the change of scenery. She noticed a wide smile spread across Zander's face as he saw her. She wasn't sure if he knew about Matthew, or the investment meeting. Nathan didn't gossip and the only person she'd told about her background was Patrice. She waved though didn't linger to chat.

Nathan was always so upbeat. He had a way of sauntering into a room with an expression like he had a secret. Lexi realized he probably had plenty.

"Matthew aka Mr. Carl Forbes should be sitting around feeling completely out of his depth and crapping himself right now."

Lexi looked shocked that he was able to joke about it. "Aren't you worried?"

"His fake persona won't stand up to much scrutiny. They will want to know more than he's willing to tell them. But he's meeting with an investment panel not the CIA. And Lexi, I'm not trying to tell you how to feel about him, but he's not a bad guy. He made a terrible mistake, so try and remember that when he gets here. He was scared but he did this because you asked him to."

While they waited for Matthew, Lexi shared some of her findings on the positive outcomes that areas of the Volt had achieved. She hoped it could be used to sway the council's decision. There was so much she hadn't realized they did: After school programs, breakfast clubs, literacy classes. People needed the Volt.

"I don't know who actually runs this place," Lexi said, "I mean isn't there a management, a board, or a committee?"

"Good question. Ken Ferguson's death meant a lot that should have happened, didn't, so there is no one entity in charge. The Entrepreneurial Center manages the finances, and all the individual services are overseen by the City. Unfortunately, that means no one is fighting for it, well, until you came along."

Lexi looks surprised. "Me?"

Nathan smiled. "I know you don't realize it, but the fight is on because of you. If you hadn't started asking questions, had the initial meeting with Amanda and pieced things together, we might not have seen the threat that was coming."

Lexi was about to argue that Nathan would have figured it out, when Matthew arrived.

Lexi noticed the smell, Matthew had been sweating, stress sweat, she tried not to wrinkle her nose. He looked like he had been through an ordeal.

"The name's Scottish apparently. You could have told me that. A guy called Bob wanted to talk about our heritage and I didn't know what to say."

Nathan laughed. "That was the worst bit? What did you find out? Is it the Volt they are buying into?"

Matthew was flustered. "Wait a minute I have notes. Yes it's the Volt and more, but I didn't understand half of it. Here are the names of the people in the room, I managed to do that part."

Nathan and Lexi looked over the names, no surprises--no Frank but Celeste was on the list.

"Here it is, these seemed like the important parts." Matthew read, "Everything is being done with the City's agreement. No one is losing anything; they will still have the same library and garden etc. They might not be in as pretty a location or look the same and they won't all be together. It will be the Tribune of the future."

Lexi said. "What do they mean the Tribune of the future? I thought it was just the Volt?"

Matthew was not making a good job of explaining himself

and began looking through his notes again. "Let me find it." Matthew read, "They are a consortium of high-risk investors, who will buy the land and the buildings. It's like flipping houses. I underlined that part. They buy the part of town on behalf of the company who are looking for a location in the South. It's cheaper for their workers who are keen to locate here and eventually, the whole campus will move here. If they decide to go with a different town, there are many other big corporations lining up for a place like this."

Nathan looked unusually concerned. "Who, Matthew, who are they selling the town to?"

"I'm not supposed to tell anyone this part but I didn't actually sign anything. I didn't write it down, but I remember it. They showed us a 3-dimensional model of a town with a lake and high-rise condos. When I asked if it was Tribune, they said. 'No, you are looking at Glass Jelly Tribune.'"

Nathan and Lexi both gasped and Lexi said. "They're selling the town to a social media company."

"Not *a* social media company, *the* social media company, one of the biggest in the world. Good job, Matthew. Was there anything else that seemed important?" Nathan asked.

Matthew handed them a glossy brochure, attached was a card with a unique investor number. "I have three days to email them back with a decision. They seem to think I have five-million at my disposal."

Nathan said. "They've seen what I wanted them to see. Don't worry, they'll have no further interest in your alter ego once you decline the offer."

Lexi looked at Nathan. "If we have everything we need, I'm sure Matthew would like to get back to his room."

Nathan agreed, "Keep your head down for a few more days, we'll be in touch."

After Matthew left, Nathan told Lexi, "Glass Jelly will

come in and build their campus, housing costs will rise, and they will price locals out of the housing market. This is so much worse than just the Volt. We need to get our heads together; you don't have to explain who Matthew is, but we need to have a meeting and update Amanda and Zander."

Lexi agreed "We also have the race this weekend; I know it's not a big deal in the scheme of things, but I need to pull everyone back together. Though we need to be careful what we say around Patrice. Let's talk after our group run tomorrow. A brisk run will be good to clear our heads.

24

———————

Lᴇxɪ ᴡᴏʀʀɪᴇᴅ they weren't ready for the coming race. They only had two training runs left, and the race was Saturday. There was nothing to stop her from running by herself, of course. She wasn't officially their leader; she'd just taken it upon herself to keep them focused. They had so much other drama going on, though, maybe the race would be a pleasant distraction. As if by thinking it, a text appeared from Deb.

I'm not going to make it. I can't find Bella.

Lexi dialed Deb's number. She wasn't prepared to let her off the hook and knew this conversation was too complicated to continue by text. "Deb, you can't afford to miss another run. How long is it since you've seen Bella?"

"This isn't just about Patrice. I've not seen Bella for days. It's getting cooler, and she always comes in when it's cold and dark. I left the cat door unlocked all night, and got up whenever I heard anything in the hope it would be her. She didn't even come when I shook her treat jar! I searched for her this morning

147

and afternoon too. It's all a mess. Patrice, the group, and now Bella. I don't care about the race anymore."

Lexi heard genuine distress. "Look, you don't have to worry about Patrice, she's focused on running the race, and I told you I talked to her. Give her some time. I have an idea. Get yourself ready to run, I'll call you back."

Lexi met the group at Tea and Two and they agreed to her idea of running in Deb's neighborhood. Lexi did a quick recalculation to include the journey to Deb's home. "I have it figured out. When we get there, we'll plan to each take a couple of streets and search for Bella while we run. We're a team, right? Let's do this."

Lexi saw that the gesture overwhelmed Deb. Even Patrice came to help. Nathan insisted on first searching her apartment. He said Bella might be injured and have hidden somewhere. Lexi could see that the state of her place was causing Deb some embarrassment. She'd let things get in a mess over the last few days. Lexi wondered if this had been a wise idea. Was she imagining the look of smug judgement from Patrice? None of them had ever been to Patrice's home, though they had heard it was a palace, decorated to Frank's exacting directions.

Bella wasn't in the apartment. Lexi knew it'd been a long shot. She wasn't feeling hopeful about finding her on the run either, though she knew nothing of cat's habits. "Let's go, we can do a slow and extra-long run, walk when necessary and ask anyone you meet if they've seen Bella."

Lexi ran ahead, she tried to imagine where a cat would hide, she could hear Patrice shouting Bella's name and was grateful that she was taking the search seriously. One of Lexi's least favorite things to do was to talk to strangers. There were few people out and about, so she felt she owed it to Deb to ask those she saw if they'd seen the cat. People were wary, they either thought she was trying to give them a cat or she was a serial killer. Well, she'd tried. There was no sign of Bella.

As the group ran back towards Deb's apartment, Nathan told them about Matthew's meeting. A run was always a good place to share information, and they were careful to be out of Patrice's earshot. Deb and Amanda didn't understand why his cloak and dagger approach was necessary. When he told them about the development plans, they rethought their assertion. Deb momentarily forgot about the reason for their run and that she was supposed to be being on the down low. "This is some serious shit. I mean, they have a lot at stake here." Suddenly, she remembered her missing cat. "What if they took Bella?"

Lexi frowned. "I think we might be getting ahead of ourselves here. They are property developers, not gangsters, and why would they target Bella?"

Patrice had caught up with them and overheard the last part. "Developers wouldn't, but someone else might." They stopped to rest at a park. Patrice sat on a bench and took a deep breath, closing her eyes. "Frank doesn't like people to cross him, I told him I believe him about Deb, and that I know he did what he did because he cares for me, but he thinks I shouldn't be running with you guys anymore. I had to tell him Deb was out of the group before he was okay with me coming."

Deb stood over her with her arms across her chest. "What does this have to do with Bella?"

Patrice looked up to see everyone waiting to hear the answer. She addressed the group avoiding looking directly at Deb.

"If Frank thinks he can't trust you to keep his secrets, he might send you a message." Patrice paused to compose herself, and then continued. "Frank's not a bad guy, I promise, but he's not like normal people. He likes to handle his business personally, and he's all about protecting his assets."

"Get to the point will you?" Deb almost screamed at her.

"When he and I first got together, I had a cat, Lucy. I'd been single for a long time after a nasty breakup. Frank saved me, he gave me everything, but he didn't like cats and said our lifestyle wouldn't work with an animal. I refused to give her up. She was a rescue, she'd become like my best friend. I wasn't going to take her back to the shelter."

"Soon after we moved to Tribune, I got in late from a spa day—a gift from Frank. I couldn't find her. I searched everywhere. Later he sat me down and told me she'd got out and was hit by a car. He wanted to save me from seeing her body, that it wasn't pretty. He said that she wouldn't have suffered, it would have been quick. When I asked him what he'd done with her, he got angry, said I didn't trust him, that I didn't appreciate all he did for me. He stormed out and was gone for hours. When he came back, he was calmer. He said he'd arranged for someone he knew to dispose of the body and was mad because I didn't trust him. He brought me a diamond cat pendant, saying it would help me remember her. It seemed sweet, but I always wondered... she was an indoor cat she never wanted to go out."

"The bastard, he killed your cat and now he's done something with mine?" Deb looked at Patrice with a mixture of anger and pity. "He's got you so you don't know which way is up. I've read about this shit in magazines, he's been gassing you."

Nathan unwisely butted in. "It's called gaslighting."

"I know what it's called. What has he done to my cat? Has he taken her for ransom?"

Lexi didn't know what to think. "He's not an idiot. What might he hope to achieve with a ransom?"

Patrice's expression grew ever more miserable. "Sometimes he likes people to know who is in charge, that's what he says. Be like the kid who beats up the bully first. But I don't think he would go after you."

"Let's all calm down and keep looking for Bella. I've got somewhere to be soon." Nathan, the normally chilled one of the group, was becoming flustered.

Lexi appealed to his practical side. "Nathan, will you post about Bella on some of those Glass Jelly lost pet websites? Deb, I know you have a ton of photos. Send Nathan a few to share."

Deb nodded in agreement but was still staring down at Patrice. "If I find out your nasty husband has anything to do with Bella being missing, I will tell everyone what I know about him. And you can tell him that."

25

Lexi had made good progress on the Volt project, but it was hard to separate her job from her own feelings. She must ensure that she had done the correct amount of research, find a reason the developers could close the Volt, but also why they shouldn't. For this assignment, her personal feelings were irrelevant.

Lexi needed to think, to clear her mind and plan her next move. She took a break and headed to the Volt's Atrium. The high glass ceiling created a perfect prism of soft sunlight that highlighted the jigsaw puzzle, an infuriating abstract image of various shades of blue. It was a community jigsaw. Anyone could take a turn, though hardly anyone had. It didn't look like it had been touched since she was last here. Lexi rarely made much progress unless she put everything out of her mind and sat still. It was a good meditation, even if she only found one piece that fit.

It would be impossible for most people to do what she had undertaken, just as five thousand pieces of various shades of blue would infuriate most people. Yet, Lexi was not quite like any other person. She'd learned to compartmentalize her life, to make sense of things that didn't have sense at their core.

Joshua appeared beside her and added a piece that fit first time. She was pleased to see him; he was the perfect person to talk over concepts, ideas and theories that were of no interest to the others in her small circle, well, until Nathan had come along. Zander was cool. But he preferred to talk about stories and fictional characters. She wanted to make a difference and do something tangible.

Her time at The Sanctuary was filled with books, and she had been surrounded by brilliant minds. She realized towards the end of her time there, that she was more of a subject than a patient, client, or resident. The Sanctuary was constantly conducting research, and though Lexi and the others had the best care and treatment, they were being used as lab rats. Lexi had not understood until later that a place in a therapeutic unit was not where most traumatized kids ended up. Places were rare and without money, most kids wouldn't have the opportunity. The Sanctuary was experimental. At least she didn't feel like an inmate.

She had found the real world a shock after she left, and her few years in the wilderness had almost destroyed her. She missed the protection, along with the stimulation of living in a vibrant community, even though it was an institution. It was the only home she had known for so long. Here in Tribune, she looked like she had it all together, yet her neuroses and anxieties sometime barely felt under control.

Lexi had an urge to tell Joshua what she knew about the Volt, but she wouldn't. Enough people were in the know already. Instead, she would see how far she could get with Joshua by talking big picture. She took out her notepad. "I need to prove something that will create a narrative that is not true, or that is only partly true." She drew a circle at the top of the page, inside she wrote the words:

. . .

Almost True Story

"The truth will be used to create a story based on a lie."

She drew another circle and wrote:

Damaging Lie

"I need to find a middle ground that will allow the truth to be less damaging than the lie."

She wrote in the middle of the page.

Noble lie

Joshua found another piece of the jigsaw before he slid it in its rightful place in the top right-hand corner, he asked. "What color is this piece?"

With a resigned expression, "Blue, though some people might call it turquoise, but it is still blue."

"And this one?"

"Also blue, maybe azure."

"And if we put them side by side, they would look completely different, yet they would still be blue."

"So, what? they're all true and they are all lies?"

Joshua smiled as he saw more pieces and could fill a whole satisfying corner. "They are part of a whole that tells a story. The story is more important than the individual pieces or, as some like to call them—facts. How you present the story will determine how it is received, and how wonderful that they have chosen you to tell the story, because you can frame it how you like."

"Yes, but I'm being paid to tell it the way they want." Lexi had a moment of panic when she realized she was saying too much, even when saying nothing.

"Maybe they don't know what they want."

He leaned in and whispered: "We need you. The town needs you. I can help. Lexi you can trust me. I know you have a heart for this community and especially those experiencing homelessness, we appreciate it."

Lexi was confused. "We?"

"By most definitions, though I'm luckier than most. I have a van that I sleep in, though calling it a home is a stretch. My background is only relevant in that I know this town. I still know people, and I have figured that we are probably on the same side. And cards on the table. I have been watching you for a while. Unfortunately, there might be people who make a connection between us, so we should look like we are making some serious progress completing this puzzle, or find somewhere less public to talk."

Lexi didn't know how she'd missed all this. She realized he rarely talked about himself. She'd judged him, decided that because he was clever and always well-dressed and clean-shaven, he couldn't be one of the homeless community.

"I was a journalist, a successful one. Then I got too close to a story that powerful people didn't want me to tell. They tried to close me down, and I refused to be stopped. I'd made mistakes. I had a brief fling with a woman who worked in one of the strip clubs. I only got to know her because I was helping her out with bills. I'm not making excuses, I was weak. It was over almost as quickly as it began, but someone had taken photographs. I didn't know who, or why, someone had been following me. It was the one and only time we'd been intimate and yet someone was watching. My wife was mortified and angry, though she was prepared to forgive me if I gave up the story. I refused, and she left me. I was a fool, the story went nowhere. I drank more and became depressed."

Lexi could tell that he was being truthful and felt she could trust him.

"Would it surprise you to know that the person behind my downfall was Frank Fleming?"

Although it shouldn't have come as a surprise somehow Lexi hadn't seen it coming.

Joshua's voice was calm, yet there was a pained emotion that he couldn't hide from Lexi.

"I was following him, Frank. I had a lead that he was doing something underhand, possibly paying city officials to push developments through. An instinct also convinced me he had something to do with Ken Ferguson's death. Ken was fit and well, with good eyesight. He knew to take care crossing the unlit roads outside town. They never found the car that hit him, no witnesses, but someone left him to die at the side of the road and I wanted to find out who. I wasn't sure what I was looking for, so I went old school and tailed him. I'd done a stint as a PI years ago. I hoped to see him hand over a brown paper envelope stuffed with notes or a secret meeting with a politician, but what I saw was what led to my current status."

Lexi leaned in closer, intrigued, yet worried about what she was about to learn.

"I followed him to the river and thought it was a strange place for a meeting. As I got closer, I saw he was holding one of those reusable shopping bags and it appeared to be moving. He tied the top and pulled as if making sure it was secure, and then tossed it into the river. He looked around before heading up the bank to his car. I was pretty sure he hadn't seen me, and I suspected that time was of the essence, so headed down to where he'd been. The bag not yet sunk. I waded in and dragged it out with a stick. The bag was heavy, already waterlogged, and nothing was moving. I couldn't get the top to untie and began grabbing at the bag, trying to tear it open."

Joshua looked at Lexi, and she could see he was remembering the experience vividly.

"Have you ever been in a panic and you do the opposite of what you know you should? You can't remember the best way to fix it because you are in complete paralysis?"

Lexi knew exactly what he meant. She'd experienced the

feeling when she couldn't find her wallet or thought she'd left the stove on. She would suddenly lose all sense of clarity and even the breathing exercises Lorna had taught her were no good, as she couldn't remember how to do them. Lexi tried to focus on his story and not allow her empathy to take her into her own memory of panic.

"I stopped for a moment and put my hand to the bulk in my jacket pocket, a Swiss army knife the kids bought me as a joke. I was always hopeless at anything practical. It had numerous tools and gadgets. Now to find the one that was an actual knife, I struggled to get a grip and after pulling out a corkscrew, then a magnifying glass, I came across a tiny pair of scissors. They were sharp. I ripped open the bag. Inside was a soaking wet, lifeless, dark ball of fur. As I lifted the creature's head I saw it was a cat and had the craziest idea to attempt resuscitation. I'd been on a first aid course. I guessed I could improvise. Giving a cat heart massage after breathing into its fishy mouth was not something I want to repeat, though eventually there were signs of life and the cat who we would later name Lucky, threw up her breakfast and was alive."

Lexi saw a little sign of victory in Joshua's face.

"Patrice's cat? he told her it had been hit by a car."

"I know. He told me all about it, when he threatened me about telling Patrice or attempting to return the cat. I gave the puss a new name to go with her new life."

"He knew you saw him do it?" Now things were making sense.

"I was a fool and didn't know who I was dealing with. I thought I could leverage what I knew with this fresh evidence and challenge him about his corrupt activities. I guessed it was his cat. When I challenged him, he was brazen said he would have me arrested for blackmail and if I didn't back off, he could make life very difficult for me. He made good on his promise. I was walking home one night, and someone came behind me and hit me hard on the head. Next thing, I'm being dragged out of the river, just like the cat except my lungs weren't as strong as hers. I had damage that took too long to heal, time in hospital and then rumors spread that I couldn't challenge, with no way to defend myself as I was too ill. Things unraveled I started drinking again."

Lexi noted the "again" but there was already too much to take in.

"So here we are. He ruined me. Most people know the stories were bullshit but mud sticks, and I was guilty of some of it. That's why we must be careful. I can help but I don't want him to hurt you like he did me. And he will."

Lexi stared at him in shock. "And Lucy, Lucky?"

"I didn't know what to do with her. I couldn't give her back, though I wanted to. This guy is nuts and I didn't know what he would do next. Before the attack, I kept her. I was afraid to take her to the vets in case she was chipped, and they returned her to her owner. It would all come back to me. Eventually I gave her to someone for safekeeping. Nathan has her now."

"You know Nathan?"

"Nathan took over where I left off."

Joshua added a couple more pieces to the outer edge of the jigsaw, as if he had been choosing them the whole time. Lexi and Joshua had made a show of moving pieces around the board for over thirty minutes while he told his story, they made plans to meet again. He might have fallen from grace and disappeared from the public arena, yet he'd never stopped paying attention. He still knew what was happening below Tribune's surface.

"We've already spent too long here. Have a look into the archives of the local papers, anything you can come up with about Ken Ferguson, his death and the investigation afterwards. He gave her a piece of paper. Put this number in your phone under Lucky, then swallow it. Just kidding, be careful. Talk to Nathan."

Lexi understood the stakes were higher than she'd realized, and though it scared her, it also solidified her resolve. It was no longer rumor. She couldn't allow Frank to continue to get away with his criminal behavior. Though she wondered about one thing, she'd seen no evidence of a cat at Nathan's house.

26

———

Patrice decided she should forgive Deb and, by association, the group—them more so, because she came to believe they weren't part of the subterfuge. Yet, as she had time to reflect, she revisited her decision. Frank told her more details that he said proved Deb couldn't be trusted, she had to make a choice. She couldn't believe both them and him. Someone was lying and Frank was the one she had made a vow to, not Deb.

They were enjoying what was looking like a promising romantic dinner, yet Frank still had a lot to say about Lexi. "They laugh at you, you know; call you names and comment about your weight. They think you hang with them because you aren't good enough to be with a real running group. I've had months to get to know what they think of you from Deb, and Lexi is the worst."

"I can understand why Deb would be like that, but I can't think that Lexi would be so petty, she seems to be above that kind of thing."

Frank countered, "But you were unhappy that I paid Deb, yet your buddy Lexi knew and didn't tell you."

It was true, Patrice had struggled with the knowledge that Lexi had at some point known before she did about Deb.

"Look you understand I sometimes deal with confidential deals; I can't tell you everything I know, but that Lexi, she can't be trusted."

Patrice wasn't sure what to make of it all. Frank could be hard work, demanding, though he had been so much better over the last few days. He'd brought her gifts, talked about a vacation, complimented her looks and even, atypically, instigated sex. It felt like the passion they had when they met. Maybe his possessiveness and controlling nature could be looked at another way, she was everything to him and ultimately, he would do anything to protect their relationship, even if it didn't always seem like it to those looking from the outside. He was her husband, and she needed to be loyal.

"I'm glad you're doing the race, though you should make it the last one. I'll help you find something that's a more suitable match for our lifestyle. Golf maybe?" Frank suggested.

Patrice was torn, and pondered how she might find a way of continuing running that didn't include the Tutus or doing it alone. After a couple of glasses of wine, she was wrapped in a warm and fuzzy glow, comfortable with the man she loved and wanting him to know she was on his side. She leaned over and took his hand. "You know if Deb is the only one who betrayed me, maybe there's another way I can keep running with the others. Help me to understand. What is it you think Lexi's doing that could hurt your business? If you told me what you were working on, I might be able to help. I know she's always reading and researching, and I've sometimes caught her whispering, or the conversation shuts down when she sees me. They were having some secret chats last night when we were looking for Deb's cat."

Frank's expression changed, it began with a slight tremble of the lower lip. Patrice regained her clarity and realized her mistake.

"I thought you'd agreed to stop running with them?"

"I just thought... I should have said, we only have one more run before Saturday's race, then I'll be done with them." Patrice's desire to head off the argument, to shift Frank back to his good mood, meant she kept talking. Sometimes it worked. He might forget what he was angry about.

"We changed our whole route to go searching for Deb's cat while we were running. Can you believe that? It's gone missing and Deb was all paranoid. She was even ranting that you had something to do with it."

Frank set down his wineglass. It teetered on the edge of a coaster. He grabbed it and slammed it down on the dining room table; she held her breath and waited for the onslaught that she knew was coming. How easily she'd forgotten about his temper, convincing herself each time that it was a one-off, that she was overreacting to his emotional outbursts that were about protecting their lifestyle, and their marriage. When she was in it like right now, she knew this was not normal. The sick feeling in her stomach told her it was all wrong. She was stupid to bring it up, and it unleashed a torrent of anger from Frank. Something about the look in his eye when she mentioned the cat told her he definitely knew something. Oh God, what had she done? She was going to have to tell the group that they might be in danger.

"I thought we settled this. You don't meet them anymore; you will run your race and then I don't want to hear about Deb or your silly group of runners ever again. I don't care about her cat or your cat or anybody's cat. I tried to do you a favor, find you friends and you were mad at me for that. Now it turns out they are a bunch of losers, and you still want to hang on to them. I need you to learn to do as I say."

She expected Frank would storm off to the Golf club and

come back later, but he stayed, poured himself another drink and was silent for a few more minutes. When she dared look up at him, he was smiling.

"Forget what I said. I want you to stay with your little running buddies, but there are some things I'm going to need you to do for me. Let's start by you telling me everything you know about each of them. Beginning with Lexi. What do you think she's working on? And what do you know about her that I don't?"

Patrice was scared but looked him in the eye and shook her head. She had never pushed it before. It was easier to have a quiet life and go along with his plans. She realized she didn't know how he would react if she refused him. She'd never tried. But thinking of how much the group had meant to her, how good it felt to have friends again, a life separate from him. It was time to stand up to him. "I'm not telling you any—"

Frank didn't allow her to finish, he grabbed her hair with one hand and her neck with the other. The same hands that had held her so gently now stole her breath.

"I need you to listen. And before you say anything, consider carefully where your loyalties lie." He dropped his grip on her hair to punctuate his words with painfully sharp prods to her collarbone. "This house, this charmed life you lead. It all comes from me. They belong to me, and can all be taken away." He forced her to sit while he demanded information. "What about Lexi?"

Patrice was shaken by the violence. She wanted to run, but saw she had to offer something. She didn't think anything she knew could harm Lexi. She would be betraying Lexi's confidence, but she had to protect herself. "She doesn't talk about her work, says it's confidential, but the others they seem to know it's to do with the Volt, everyone's worried about it closing, but no one tells me anything. I just sometimes overhear stuff.

She talks to the homeless guy sometimes and her name, that's not her real name." Patrice put up a hand to stop him demanding more answers. She grabbed her phone and pulled up an article she'd found after Lexi had told her about her past.

The Girl With The Body: The Tragic Story That Shocked A Town.

Frank read every detail and when he'd finished displayed a sardonic grin.

"This should help stop any plans she might have. So, what about the rest of them?"

Patrice knew little else that she could tell him about the others, though his ears pricked up at the news that Lexi was close to Nathan and the homeless guy. Maybe it would be okay, and Patrice hadn't done any damage. Still, she felt terrible. She finally saw her life clearly. She had been fooling herself about Frank. Now she needed to focus on herself and her future. Lexi had tried to warn her, but she hadn't listened. Worse, she had betrayed Lexi's secret. Patrice wondered what other lies Frank had told her that she had allowed herself to believe.

27

———

THERE WAS SO MUCH HAPPENING that it was hard to get excited about the race. Lexi was determined to put everything to one side and just run. It seemed like an excellent opportunity for the group to get together and blow off some steam. This was the first time they'd all run together, including Amanda, since the revelation of Deb working for Frank. They still hadn't brought Deb completely into the loop and Lexi knew they would need to soon. Deb had figured out that there was more going on than they were telling her.

Patrice had promised to see what she could find out about Frank's business dealings but hadn't come up with anything, and had been quiet. They met at Tea and Two and planned to walk together to the start line. Zander was waiting for them and had baked some running treats. He might not be a runner, but they still considered him part of the team.

Lexi knew he had wanted to get to know her, but the potentially disastrous future for the Volt and his business had made their personal lives less of a priority. They accepted the snacks and Nathan ate his immediately. He'd bought a registration and was officially running the race. They all agreed he shouldn't draw attention to himself; he'd even changed his hair to its original brown, the spiky blond making him stand out.

They needed time to think. They would run the race and then come back together tomorrow to talk about what they knew between them. There was barely a plan to save the Volt, and Lexi still had to submit her report.

Patrice and Lexi kept their distance from each other. Deb nudged Lexi to make sure she had seen the Tutus lined up at the front. They had gone with an early winter wonderland theme. Sparkly sheer tutus, white running leggings and matching leotards. Deb was feeling in a particularly bitchy mood. "Of course, they've topped the look off with tiaras because they are all such princesses. They look like they should be in a 1980s fitness video rather than a race."

Lexi was non-committal. She was trying not to allow her dislike of the Tutus, and especially Celeste, to spoil her day. She would take the higher ground, each to their own. Though as she had the thought, she realized Celeste wasn't with them. That was unusual, she usually took any opportunity to lap up the limelight. If Celeste was going to run, she'd better hurry up.

It began to rain a little. This was unexpected. The forecast had been for the rain to come later in the day. As the raindrops began to get bigger, Lexi saw the crowd part at the front and Celeste arrived to join her group. By the time the anthem had been sung and the race was about to begin, the Tutus shiny costumes were starting to look waterlogged. They were not designed for wet weather. Celeste's normally glossy mane of highlighted tresses looked stringy. She was visibly annoyed. Though Lexi and the group didn't like running in the rain, they didn't dress for style, so were unworried by a pop-up shower, although this was looking more like a serious downpour.

Lexi had encouraged them to move further towards the front instead of hiding at the back, so they were perfectly placed to see the fun that unfolded. As the rain continued to pour, the Tutus' outfits became more and more sheer. By the time the group heard the starting pistol, the tutus appeared naked from the waist up, the short tutus made from pearlescent silk rather than the usual netting shriveled in the rain. Celeste looked around desperately, maybe she hoped to see one of her minions, who would come to her aid with a rain jacket to preserve her modesty. No one was forthcoming.

The start line antics spurred the group on, and their camaraderie helped them to ignore the rain. They ran faster and harder than they might have expected, and they were thoroughly soaked by the time they reached the finish line. The squelch of their feet in their running shoes and a few blisters did not take away from the personal record for each of them, and the heavy medal they would refuse to take off all day.

They waited to see what had happened to the Tutus, who were nowhere to be seen. The mayor and other dignitaries were talking in hushed tones. The group ate their post-race bananas and were heading to Tea and Two when they saw the bedraggled bunch return. They lumbered to the finish line wrapped in silver thermal blankets, looking dejected and miserable. Lexi wondered why they didn't just get a ride home and forget the race. She guessed Celeste would not be beaten. She needed a win, even if it was a bad one.

The group had a wonderful breakfast of homemade oatmeal, coffee, hot chocolate and, of course, a selection of toast and toppings. Zander brought them towels, although they had been smart enough to bring a change of clothes.

When the news coverage of the race came on the local morning news, Zander turned up the sound, making an exception to the no TV rule. The camera panned to the Tutus. In their confusion and embarrassment at their predicament, they took a wrong turn and soon they were hopelessly lost. A drone filming aerial footage of the race took a detour and followed the Tutus' torturous trek through the additional and unnecessary miles. The Tutus kept running, the rain never let up, and by the time most others had reached the finish line, they were still a couple of miles away. During the time it had taken for the group to eat their breakfast, a video of the footage was uploaded to Glass Jelly and already shared thousands of times. Playing over a well-known song used by striptease artists, it showed them running in their soaked outfits. They wandered through a local housing project where residents delighted in mocking them. Another speeded-up version of their return journey was even funnier. The group laughed until they cried.

Zander watched the scenes with bemusement," I know they are a bit snooty and ridiculous, but dare I ask? Why do you all turn into mean girls around the Tutus, no offense Nathan. What did they ever do to you?"

Nathan laughed harder, and Amanda and Lexi looked suitably chastised. Deb rejected the criticism, "I might not be Patrice's best friend, but I'm with her on what she said about Celeste. It applies to the others, too. They're like the bullies in high school—they probably *were* bullies—and if karma comes for them, I'm here for it with popcorn. It's a shame Patrice wasn't here to enjoy the show with us. Do you think we'll see her again?"

Lexi had been wondering the same thing. "Patrice? Not if Frank gets his way. She said he didn't want her to run with us anymore."

Though it had been a welcome change from their own drama, Lexi worried that the public embarrassment of the Tutus would cause problems. Celeste wasn't a woman you wanted to cross and though no one could control the weather, she wondered if she would be looking for someone to blame. Then she stopped herself. She was overthinking again and putting herself at the heart of imaginary problems.

The fun of the race wore off. They each had their own struggles. Deb had still not found Bella and was giving up hope. Lexi had to finish her report and her head wasn't in it. Matthew, and his role in her mother's death was never far from her thoughts. She still didn't know how to feel about that. Knowing he was around town was distracting. She hoped that Amanda and Nathan had made progress on saving the Volt, and possibly the town. Now the race was out of the way she had to see if there was anything else she could do to help. She wasn't sure she had been much use and the Council meeting was next week.

Lexi headed home. She'd enjoyed the morning but was uncomfortable being sweaty in public. Though she'd been grateful for the dry clothes she'd been able to change into at the Volt. Another innovative idea: the provision of lockers for the homeless to keep their valuables and personal documents somewhere safe. Thankfully, there were a few for runners too.

The walkability and relative safety had been a factor in her decision to stay in Tribune. Though she could drive, it was another anxiety she hadn't got over. Much better to walk when she could. She was never happier than when she entered her pristine apartment after exercise. As she approached it this time, she sensed something wasn't quite right.

A smudge of dirt on a doorframe might not have alerted someone less obsessed with detail, but Lexi saw it immediately. She had created her surroundings to be exactly how she wanted to live, and that meant keeping them that way. She paid a window cleaner to maintain the cleanliness of not only the glass but also the external woodwork, siding and doorframes. Someone had been here.

The door was locked, it looked as if someone had opened it

and relocked it. Her front door was visible from the street, so she was unsure whether to go inside or call someone. She went around the back and looked through the window. She crouched down and raised her head to see through the blinds. It didn't look like anyone was inside. She returned to the front and opened the door.

The first thing that hit her was the smell. A definite odor: unmistakably excrement. She covered her mouth with her jacket and looked around. A trail of shit was evident throughout the apartment, yet the intruder had disturbed nothing else. The dirty trail quickly led to the answer.

Before she did anything else; she called Deb. She could tell from the background noise that she was still at the Volt. "I need you to stop what you're doing and get over to my place right now. Bring Nathan. He knows where I live."

Ten minutes later, they arrived. Deb had never been inside Lexi's apartment but didn't have time to admire it. The first thing she saw was the cat-shit. Her expression changed from confusion to delight as Lexi pointed to the bookcase. Hiding under the smallest space that would have seemed impossible to accommodate even a mouse, was Bella.

"What the, how? I don't understand." Deb reached down and coaxed Bella out as she stared from Lexi to Nathan.

Lexi threw up her hands. "We have at least two problems. Figuring out who broke into my apartment to deliver your cat, and how to clean up this shit."

Deb had tears in her eyes as she held Bella and inspected her for any sign of injury. "She only did it because she was scared, she's a very clean cat."

Nathan looked worried. "This is a message, and though it looks like they haven't done the cat any harm, they've been able to get into both of your apartments unseen. Let's get this place cleaned up while we think."

As Lexi went to check the rest of the apartment, she saw something else. Laying on her pillow was a Polaroid photograph, the type instantly developed from the camera. It was a photograph of Bella inside a cage. She turned it over to find a small sticky note attached, with the scrawled words.

Only cats have nine lives.

Deb and Nathan were focused on scraping up the vomit they had discovered under the furniture. As they looked up, Lexi handed Nathan the photo with a shaking hand. What had in the moments before seemed so ridiculous, almost a prank, now had become threatening and personal. Nathan took a closeup of the photograph and then ran it through an app on his phone. "Was hoping I could detect something in the background, but it looks like they kept her in some sort of warehouse, poor thing."

Lexi leaned in. "Let me see something." She took Nathan's phone, compared the photo to the image on the screen and zoomed in, "Look! in her eye." Nathan and Deb squinted to see what Lexi was looking at. Bella was clearly looking at the person holding the camera, her eyes wide with fear, reflected in one of them was a white shape.

Nathan became animated "That's the downtown Church, the old one. If I'm not mistaken, there is a big house opposite. They must have left a door open to get light in for the photo. If it's not there I'm not sure, that area is mainly residential."

Deb looked less convinced. "Or is it the back side of the Church, would the tower look the same from both sides? What's on the other side?"

Nathan's eyes darted around as he located the map in his brain: "That's where the tiny houses are, doesn't Zander live in one?"

Lexi felt less fraught, and was ready for a fight. "We need to get over there and find out who is trying to scare me off. It makes little sense though. If it's the developers, they could just fire me and tie me up in legal knots until they've got what they want."

Nathan emptied the bucket he had been using and collected the soiled paper towels. "It would be better if I went. They know you two are connected. Though whoever it is, they could be watching us. They knew you were out this morning. If you can finish up here, I will ride my bike over and look around."

In Deb's arms, Bella looked less terrified, and Lexi kept one eye on her to make sure she left no more evidence of her visit. Thank goodness her apartment had little in the way of soft furnishings or carpet. She would have to open all the windows, maybe even pay a cleaning service to sanitize the place. It wasn't the cat's fault, but she was furious, it was as if her enemies knew exactly how to rattle her.

28

———

Lexi loved walking, though she was sore from yesterday's race and on this evening she was ill-equipped. A low fog had hidden the setting sun, and her thin jacket did little to keep out the cold. She'd promised Lorna that she would check in regularly during this unusual time, but the walk to Lorna's office felt somehow ominous. She realized the mist clinging to her hair would make her look disheveled by the time she arrived. Lexi changed her mind about walking and headed back the way she came to get her car.

Lexi had allowed a misconception regarding her habit of walking everywhere. Her friends believed it was for fitness or environmental reasons. Though partly true, she had left it too late to admit that she owned a car she rarely drove. That would mean explaining more than she wanted to about her anxiety.

Lorna was one of the few people who knew and so arriving by car would not be a big surprise. It mainly sat in a rented garage covered in a tarp. Lexi always made sure it was in a drivable condition, turning the engine over every now and again and occasionally driving the brief journey to the business district when she had meetings. The alternative—to take a cab

173

or ride service had been ruined by a particularly messy car. It looked like the driver lived in it and the remnants of his takeaways were evident, if not by sight, certainly by smell. She also found small talk torturous. Facing her driving phobia was the lesser of two evils. Even though driving was an activity she only forced herself to do on a handful of occasions, she was glad to have risked it to avoid what she could only describe as a feeling of fear and dread.

Once in the session with Lorna, Lexi avoided bringing up her feelings of dread, knowing it would have resulted in a protracted discussion about trusting her gut.

"Lexi, I know you've said you can't talk about your current work. Remember, anything you tell me is confidential. You can talk about the challenges you're facing and talk through any strategies if it might help you clarify your thoughts."

Lexi sank into the chair and sighed. "You got me into this mess Lorna."

"How so?"

"You convinced me to connect with people, and now I am in the unexpected position of caring about them. This town has some very bad people in power. They are going to destroy everything that makes it worth living here. I have to decide if I stand up to them and put myself in the firing line or walk away and look after myself."

"Lexi, you know I can't support you putting yourself in danger, but there may be other ways you can help the town. You also need to remember that you don't have to do everything alone. You always try to struggle through, even when there are people ready and willing to help. Think about your allies and learn to trust them."

Lexi wanted to tell Lorna that she didn't need this advice, that she'd finally found people she trusted. Yet it felt risky, as if saying it out loud would jinx it, that her friends would then let her down.

Lorna paused before she continued. "Did you want to talk about Matthew?"

"I'm going to let that sit for a while longer. It's come at the worst possible time. He was easier to manage as a monster in my head. I don't know what to do with the real-life pathetic version."

Lorna didn't push further.

Lexi left the office and walked quickly along the sidewalk to the side street where she'd parked. Her soft-soled boots made no sound on the pavement, and she became aware of other footsteps, they were behind her or close by. She walked faster and almost reached the car, still trying to figure out the direction the steps were coming from. She heard car tires crunching on the gravel beside her. The choice between running and attempting to unlock the car was taken from her. She could not move fast enough to do either. As the footsteps caught up to her, the car stopped, and a door opened. Both these things happened simultaneously.

She was suddenly looking at Frank Fleming. "Get in."

29

———

THE MAN who followed her opened the car's rear door, then switched places with Frank. Lexi reluctantly climbed in the sedan's back seat. Frank joined her. She was afraid but less than she would have expected. Lexi realized that she probably could have still run, but she wanted this over with. Her instinct that danger was looming had been correct, she was almost relieved that it was finally here.

"Alexandra King, I believe."

Lexi took a sharp intake of breath. This was not what she had been expecting. She tried to speak, but he pushed two fingers onto her lips and yelled in her face.

"Nice name. It would be a shame if everyone knew you're the fruit loop who's been locked up for years. Who would trust you to do important work for them if they knew you were a crazy loser?"

Frank moved his hand to the back of her head and pushed her face into the seat. The smell of leather cleaner filled her nose as he continued to yell at her. "Did you come back to take revenge on whoever you think killed your mommy? I don't know what you are up to, but I know we paid you to do a job, yet you are hanging out with characters who don't have my best interests at heart. I want you to cease and desist." He pushed her head harder into the leather emphasizing the word desist. "Or you might wish you were back in that loony bin. I am looking out for this town I'm going to make it better. Oh, and if you decide to share any stories with my wife, you won't be staying around for long."

Lexi's fear grew as she realized Frank was as dangerous as she had been warned. She never expected that he would dare lay a finger on her. She had the taste of chemicals in her mouth and the smell of Frank's cologne in her nose. She felt sick.

The car stopped. Lexi hadn't been aware it was moving; she'd been focused on breathing. As Frank let her up, she realized she was on the other side of town. The driver jumped out and dragged her out of the car. She landed on her hands and knew there would be grazes, maybe worse.

As the driver returned to the car, Frank rolled down his window. "The homeless guy you've taken pity on, take a lesson from him. He used to have a life. He thought he could cross me, and you see how he ended up."

Before Lexi could even process what had happened, the car sped off and they were gone. Lexi was shaken and upset at her weakness. She had no skills to fight back. She'd experienced bullying before, but nothing like this. Frank wasn't a schoolyard bully who would back down. He was reckless and unhinged—a psychopath. Someone who would attempt to drown a cat and destroy a person's life probably had no limits.

Lexi realized she needed help. As well as her sore hands, her leg hurt. She couldn't make the long walk back to her car. She had to think of who to call. She needed to warn Deb who they were dealing with, and she would have to trust Deb with her past. It seemed it was about to become public knowledge whatever she did.

She called, and Deb was with her within fifteen minutes.

"Frank did this? Oh, Lexi, what is going on?" Deb moved towards her, and Lexi realized she was about to hug her. She raised her bloody hands. "It's okay, just help me get cleaned up."

Lexi agreed to go to Deb's apartment. She was exhausted and shaken. She remembered Lorna's advice about accepting help. Deb gently cleaned away the grit and blood from her hands and listened while Lexi shared the short version of her history, and how Frank now knew.

"Well, of course, Patrice never told me. We're barely speaking. But she went and told Frank. What was she thinking? I thought she was on our side. I remembered the story of the girl with the body, we prayed for her as kids. I don't remember the doctor being part of the story, though. He's helping you? This is some next level spy shit."

"What else do you know about Frank," Lexi asked. "What does he do? Who is he involved with and what else did he have you doing for him?"

"I guess as we have both signed some sort of agreement that involves Frank, we have to trust each other. You know about the Patrice story, that's where it started. Then he demanded to know who she talked to, what she said about him. I tried to blow it off, but it became more difficult to be around her, I felt so guilty. I bet he hasn't told her that part."

"Did he have you doing anything shady?"

"Sometimes I dropped off packages. I joked they better not be drugs; he said they were legal documents. The weird thing was, I went more than once to the 'gentleman's club' on the edge of town, and one time I peeked inside the package. I thought, if it was drugs, I wasn't prepared to go to jail for him."

"Hang on, you were taking packages to the strip club on behalf of Frank? What did you find?"

"Now this, I think, is why he didn't want to let me off the

hook. He guessed I had looked. I resealed the package, but maybe someone could tell. It was full of fake ID's—of girls."

Lexi was beginning to see what kind of man Frank was. "Maybe he's providing IDs for underage girls to work in the club. It all seems random though, for a property developer."

Deb tapped her head. "Or maybe he's doing favors for someone else in return for other shady dealings. Everyone keeps their hands clean, and they have idiots like me running around."

The doorbell rang, and Deb let Nathan in. "I hope you don't mind. I called him. We need a second opinion—about everything."

Nathan looked at Lexi's hands then asked. "And how's your leg? Deb said you couldn't walk easily."

"I fell hard on my knee. It's not so bad. Good thing we don't have a race this week."

"So now will you believe me that Frank is a gangster rather than the devoted husband and business executive you thought he was? Oh and Deb, the cat's eating your mail."

Deb pulled the envelope from Bella. "I'm glad to have her home, but damn, this cat is obsessed with eating cardboard and this junk mail gets bigger and more expensive looking by the day. What a waste."

Lexi updated Nathan on her misadventure and Deb brought them tea. Lexi was seeing her in a new light, the nurturing side of Deb was endearing, she watched her talk to Bella while she inspected the ripped envelope. "Did you do this? I see that innocent face, well someone ate the corner of this envelope." Deb stopped talking to the cat and said to herself. "What is this?"

She ripped the portion that was still sealed and tipped out the contents—a small pile of photographs. As they fell, Lexi saw that one had landed face up, it depicted Deb in full-color, a close-up of her engaging in an unmistakable act of graphic sex.

Lexi and Nathan were silent as she slowly assembled the pile on the coffee table, all images of her, in various stages of exposure with a man. She looked at them and then turned her attention back to the envelope, after looking inside, she pulled out a small slip of paper.

She covered the photographs with the envelope and then wordlessly handed the paper to Lexi. There was just one word —*Shhhh!*

"He's blackmailing you. Or someone is. I mean, I can see it would be embarrassing, but you're not married so who's going to care?"

Deb looked exhausted, even thinking about what she had to say. "This is a particularly backward area regarding a women's right to do what she wants with her body. Some people see Margaret Atwood's 'The Handmaid's Tale' as aspirational. I have clients who made me sign a morality clause."

"A what?" Lexi stared in disbelief.

"And you know I'm widowed, right? The family of my dead husband are religious, the good, nice kind, not the crazies, I would hate them to see these photos. Frank knows about my background; he got the information out of me when I thought I could trust him. I bet this is him. I will struggle to find work here if these photos get out."

Nathan took Deb's hand. "What you are doing in these photographs is not illegal, blackmail is." Don't touch them again. We might be able to get some DNA from them. Lexi, give me your keys I'm going to check on your car and move it back to the garage. We all need to be very careful from here on out, and we need a meeting to share what we know."

Lexi looked at her hands. "I have a meeting with the company I work for tomorrow. What will they think?"

Nathan smiled. "Let's plan to meet after that. I'll contact everyone else. Come on Lexi, I'll take you home first.

30

————

Nathan drove Lexi home. He refused to leave her alone. "Zander is on his way over."

"What? No, there's no need. I don't like people being in here."

"Lexi, it's not that I think you need a man. Amanda is at home with her family. Deb is scared out of her wits, and I need to know you're safe. I have to do some more work; we're running out of time. Frank thinks he's scared us off. That will not happen. Though we don't know what else he might do. You need someone here."

Zander arrived with food. Even though she wasn't hungry, she was grateful. She'd never spent much time alone with him, and this was not how she imagined it would be. Food would at least give them something to do. Zander was also aware of the awkwardness of the situation. "You don't have to stay up with me. If you want to go to sleep, or take a bath, I'm just here for security. Though don't tell Nathan I'm more of a lover than a fighter. Oh sorry, I didn't mean...."

Lexi laughed at his discomfort. "Oh, sit down and stop

fussing. Let me get plates for the cake. Please tell me you brought cake?"

She returned with plates and two beers.

"I don't have house guests, so this is what hospitality looks like. You can stay until it gets light." Lexi bit into a slice of Zander's Lemon Drizzle cake. "Do you always have a cake ready for an occasion such as this?"

Zander smiled. "I don't have occasions such as this, well I didn't until I met you. Oh, and I must remind you it's around a month since we talked about a date and neither of us is in jail and cake is not a date, so you owe me an occasion such as a date."

"But I did literally get kidnapped, that's almost worse than jail. You do realize I was bundled into the back of a car."

"Are you okay?"

"I was scared. Now I'm angry. My security has been compromised. Frank made some outrageous mischaracterizations of me and my background. You know, don't you, about me? My history?"

Zander gave a resigned smile. "I've had the edited highlights, we're at a stage where we need to be honest. We've been thrown together and have a common goal. Nathan told me what he thought I needed to know. It's better if there aren't too many surprises. If you don't want to fill me in on the details, that's fine with me."

"Frank said I was in a loony bin—his words. I'd rather you know my version. I'm tired but doubt I will sleep for a while, so let me tell you a little of my story. That I had been institutionalized against my will is a long way from the truth. I spent years at a therapeutic facility—The Sanctuary—and it was the happiest time of my life." She allowed herself to luxuriate in happy memories.

"You know I was found with the body of my mother, that's

the part the papers talk about. What came after is what Frank is referring to. No one knew what to do with me. There was a lot of blame between the housing development where I was found and the hospital who messed up. I was five years old with too much mental and emotional trauma to be fostered with a regular family. My Aunt Regina, my mom's sister, wasn't equipped to care for me. The hospital settled before anyone even mentioned a lawsuit. They investigated and found serious failures in their management. They set up a trust fund for me, enough to allow me to find my way in life with some financial support. Someone at the hospital must have had a connection because The Sanctuary rarely had openings."

Zander asked, "So your aunt never wanted to take you?"

"She tried, but I needed professional help. I wouldn't eat, and I was obsessed with cleanliness." Lexi looked around at her pristine apartment. "Go figure."

"Was there no one else, did you have a dad?"

"I never knew my father. There was only my mom's abusive boyfriend, who we were hiding out from in my aunt's apartment. So no, there was no one else. The Sanctuary was seen as the best solution. It had unparalleled success in helping victims of kidnappings, trafficking and long-term abuse. They also took high paying clients and children of celebrities. The remote location meant it could protect the children from the paparazzi. We took a tour; I remember some of it. It felt like heaven: a sleek, pristine facility, airy ceilings, no dirt, no unpleasant smells. It was the perfect antidote to the disgusting setting where they'd found me in. I moved in shortly after my doctor established I'd suffered no permanent physical damage. They left the door open for me to be returned to Regina's care once I was healed. I never wanted to leave. As I grew, I assisted, and I was open to being the guinea pig for all the techniques they experimented with."

"So, you lived there for all of your childhood, weren't you lonely I mean for an actual family?"

"It seemed normal to me. I guess that's why I find it hard to connect, to make friends, why I never have. But I have a family. Let me tell you about my little brother."

31

ZANDER PLACED the empty beer bottle he'd been cradling on to the silver coaster protecting the pale-colored coffee table. "A brother that wasn't in Nathan's information?"

Lexi smiled. "Not biologically, but we shared the same home for a while. Children often arrived at their most terrified and vulnerable, they found hiding places. Remi had hidden in a high closet, a warm and cozy blanket storage area in the laundry room. I was chosen to be his first contact. My job was not to coax him out, but to be there if he needed anything. I brought snacks and read him stories. I told him about life at The Sanctuary, that I'd been afraid when I arrived and that it was a good place. I asked the chef to cook a pizza. His family had said it was his favorite. As the smell wafted up towards him, he finally came out of his hiding place."

Zander asked. "His family? So what was he doing there?"

"Remi was a talented child with a beautiful singing voice. Winning a TV talent show was a dream come true. His family supported him in pursuing his bright future. Then suddenly he was locked into recording deals and promotional activities before they understood the implications of a life in the spotlight. His parents knew the reality of racism, of course, yet the vitriol towards Remi, a child born in this country who had known nowhere else, was horrifying. Online trolls made his life such hell that he had decided he didn't want to live anymore. The recording company attempted to shield him. He was a commodity and they needed to make back the money invested in him. But he was too young, too fragile. Each day brought fresh layers of hatred towards him. It mystified everyone why he was being singled out.

"The death threats and nasty comments led back to one source. The runner-up in the contest, a girl who many expected to win. She came from a family with money and connections. They unleashed hell on this young boy of Indian descent who the judges had deemed more talented than their peach of a girl. By the time the scandal was uncovered, Remi was utterly broken. The Sanctuary was the recording company's last chance of recouping their investment. The Sanctuary only agreed to accept Remi as a resident after they persuaded the recording company to loosen the contractual agreements. He would not perform in public until he was completely well.

"It took almost a full year for Remi to rediscover his sparkle. I worked with him on his therapy. He disappeared from social media and focused on his journey to wellness. I grew to love him like a brother. When he left, he was no longer haunted or scared. He returned for regular visits and ongoing therapy.

"He returned to his singing career and is the face for an anti-bullying campaign that promotes kindness and unity. He is a success story, and I know without arrogance that I was part of it."

"Are you still in touch?"

"We talk regularly though he's often on tour or recording. I have an open invite to be his guest at his shows, but the crowds and noise are too much for me and flying, airplanes full of germs, hmm no thank you. I wish he was here, I know he'd come. I would only have to ask, but he has an army of people who rely on him and what good would dragging him away do?

32

———

LEXI THOUGHT ABOUT WEARING GLOVES, but that would look even stranger than her grazed and bruised hands. Underosa who were now her only client, wanted to talk about the report they had commissioned on the Volt. Lexi had emailed it end of day on Friday, but presumed they must have follow-up questions. She'd never been so glad to be finished with an assignment. She could now get on with the work of helping save the very thing her report may have damned. It was as balanced as she could make it, but also included "serious environmental concerns" with information provided by Amanda. She also argued that The Volt was created out of a spirit of community. Ken Ferguson gave the money in good faith, and even though his untimely death meant there was no legal reason the Volt could not be broken up and moved, there was a moral one.

Lexi prided herself on delivering her work ahead of time, with the exact amount of detail required. She was confident she'd given them what they needed. Amanda was still working behind the scenes and said she had some ideas that might stall any immediate construction. She wasn't ready to share with the group until she'd done more research. Lexi had no idea how confident to feel.

Celeste came into the reception area. "Lexi, please head to the office and wait for me there."

Lexi complied; It was fourteen minutes before Celeste returned. She looked serious.

"Lexi, I understand that you've always done good work for the company, yet we feel your behavior on this project has been less than professional. If the client wanted to, they could probably sue you. We've convinced them not to, but they are our client and if they believe that you have even broken the spirit of the agreement, it would be wise for you to go quietly before it costs you more than you can afford. Underosa Communications is in the unenviable position of being stuck in the middle."

Lexi considered interrupting, though she had no way of knowing what Celeste knew or what Frank had told her. She wasn't about to give Celeste any more ammunition.

"We have also learned that you have been working for us under a false identity which..."

Lexi interrupted, "Lexi Weaver is my legal name."

Celeste waved her hand, "You have been duplicitous, and we can't have your behavior affecting our reputation. We are therefore terminating our agreement. You will receive your fee but there will be no bonus. Let me remind you of the legally binding agreement that stands. Security will show you out."

As she left, Celeste added, "Your hands. You must have taken a tumble; you should be more careful."

Lexi stood on the sidewalk frozen in shock, bewildered at being treated with such contempt. She felt powerless, she wanted to go back inside, ask to speak to someone else, one of the managers she'd worked with before who had always treated her fairly. Though she knew that if she tried to speak, her mouth would contort and she would dissolve into tears. She wasn't someone who cried easily but when treated unfairly, it was an involuntary response she couldn't fight. It was the injustice, that they could fire her in such a matter-of-fact way, but there was something else. Lexi was devastated to realize, Celeste had seen her injured hands. Did she know what Frank has done? What Frank was capable of.

33

Feelings of despair and depression were not new to Lexi, yet this feeling of utter hopelessness was different. She was now without paid work, and the past that she had worked hard to leave behind would soon be common knowledge. Frank was out to destroy her and the autonomy that she'd enjoyed. She had no idea what Frank's next move might be, or what else he knew. Her report was probably good enough to convince the council. It wouldn't sell the town on the idea of the development, but with whatever else they had, it added ammunition to the wrong side. Maybe she couldn't do anything. She could admit defeat and move on somewhere else.

She was lost in these thoughts when her phone began pinging.

Amanda: *Call me.*
Nathan: *We need to talk.*

There was apparently a lot to discuss. Lexi hadn't updated them on anything. It crossed her mind that none of them had a normal day job. Thankfully, this meant they could meet in the middle of a weekday.

The Volt had a choice of different entrances. They could enter via the library, or Tea and Two, the Eden had an entrance as did the Harbor. They decided that the Harbor's laundry and shower facility was somewhere no one they were concerned about seeing them would hang out. The disdain that some of the town's well-heeled residents had for those who were struggling was well documented in the Trib Trib's letter's page and the local neighborhood Glass Jelly pages.

One by one, her friends appeared. Zander showed up with a tray of drinks. As Lexi reached for a coffee, she winced, and Nathan noticed the still fresh grazes and cuts on her hands. "Lexi you have updates?"

"Most of you know that Frank and his thug friend gave me a warning." She saw that Zander seethed at the mention of Frank laying a hand on her. "He also got me fired." Lexi filled them in, including the story about Patrice's cat.

Nathan was the only one who wasn't particularly shocked. He apprised them on Glass Jelly's involvement. Deb didn't at first understand the implications.

Lexi spelled out her fears. "This is a massive deal. They don't just want the Volt they want a good chunk of the town, and the meeting to approve the first phase is tonight. If Frank is prepared to resort to violence, what else might he do?"

Amanda spoke next. "If their plans go ahead, the massive construction will do irreversible damage to the local wildlife. I've been working on something that can buy us some time. Does anyone else have anything new?"

Lexi felt guilty, she'd failed them. She'd done barely anything to save the Volt. Even Lorna had offered some ideas. Lexi had her head so full of other stuff she couldn't come up with anything. No one else volunteered information so Amanda continued.

"Nathan, I need you to fill me in on everything you know, I've only got a few hours to put it all together. Make sure you're all at tonight's council meeting. Be prepared to ask questions. I'll have pointers for you."

Deb rolled her eyes to the ceiling and whistled. "So, don't I get a job? You know I'm not working for Frank anymore, right?"

Nathan looked at Lexi, then back at Deb. "You're not going to like this Deb, but you need to find Patrice and talk to her. It's time she knew the full extent of what a dangerous man she's married to, tell her what he did to Lexi and her cat."

Deb said, "I haven't heard from her since the race. I doubt she'll talk to me."

Deb's phone pinged. Nathan had sent her a photo of Lucky.

"Send her this, see if she recognizes her resurrected cat, then get her to come here before the meeting and make sure she doesn't tell Frank anything."

Amanda stood up to leave. "Okay, let's all meet back here at five o'clock. That should give me enough time. Be ready to take notes."

Lexi remembered her question about the cat. "Nathan, you still have Lucky? I don't remember seeing a cat at your house."

Nathan laughed. "Like me, my house has hidden depths. I don't share them all at once." Nathan always made Lexi smile. she was so grateful for him, for all of them.

As everyone was preparing to leave, Nathan spoke up. "Has anyone heard from Matthew? I haven't seen him since we met after the investment meeting. That was over a week ago, and he's not answering my calls."

Lexi was the only one to answer. "No one else was in contact with him, maybe now he's done what he came for he will have headed back." As Lexi said the words, she knew she didn't believe them. She had tried to convince herself that she didn't care about Matthew, but she had a gnawing thought that he might be in trouble.

Deb said. "If Frank was prepared to throw you out of a car and get you fired, I don't like to think what he might do to this Matthew guy if he finds out he was helping us."

Nathan paused. "He doesn't know anyone here, if anything happened to him no one other than us would miss him."

"I guess we owe it to him to make sure he's all right. I got him into this." Lexi stood and nodded to Zander. "Come on, let's go see if he's at the hotel. Nathan you're working with Amanda, right? Call us if you see Matthew or anything suspicious."

Lexi realized she didn't know how they were going to get downtown, she didn't want to drive, not with a passenger, that would double her driving anxiety. "Zander do you happen to have a vehicle?"

Zander laughed. "Does this not very successful business owner have a vehicle? Well yes how do you think I get supplies?"

Lexi slapped her forehead. "Well, d'oh, I thought you got deliveries directly from the George Orwell Appreciation Society."

Lexi was pleased to discover that Zander had a very clean minivan that he used for the business. It included no air fresheners, no ornaments on the dashboard, no food wrappers. He smiled as he saw her inspecting and then looked serious.

"Do you think he will be okay? I don't know much about him but if Frank's as bad as everyone says, I can see why you are worried."

"I have no idea what to think to be honest." Lexi admitted.

As they arrived at the hotel Zander suggested. "Let me go

see what I can find out. I know some of the managers here, the desk clerk might not give out information."

Lexi agreed and explored the opulent hotel lobby.

Zander returned with news. "He's not here right now but he's still staying here, he's been coming and going."

Lexi was relieved. "Well that's something I guess."

At 5:00 pm they met at Tea and Two. Everyone but Patrice and Matthew were there, including some additions, Joshua and Lorna. Lexi introduced them. "Some of you know Joshua, he unfortunately experienced being on the wrong side of Frank. And this is Lorna, a mental health professional who will be an expert witness."

Zander explained "We didn't find Matthew, but he hasn't checked out of the hotel and someone saw him yesterday."

Nathan looked relieved. "Let's set aside our concern for now. We've only got a couple of hours to put all of this together, and we need to focus on the meeting. I don't think Frank knows who Matthew is."

An unexpected voice interjected, "Frank knows a lot more than you think. But before we get into that, is this true?" She held up her phone showing the photograph of her long-lost cat. "What Deb said, is it true? Is Lucy alive? If you tricked me to get me here, I will be going straight back out again."

All eyes turned to look at Patrice. She had directed her question to Nathan, but Joshua answered. "It's true, ma'am, I pulled the kitty out of the river myself. Your husband left your cat to drown. Later he did the same to me."

Patrice looked strange. She had not made the normal effort with her makeup, and Lexi realized that there was something very wrong. "Patrice, are you okay? What happened? What's wrong with your neck?"

"I'm fine. Frank and I had a fight. He made me tell him

about you. I'm so sorry. I know none of you like him or trust him, and you are right."

Lexi didn't understand, "Told him what?"

Patrice answered, "About your background. He's furious. I don't know exactly what's going on. He thinks you might mess up a deal he's involved in. He doesn't trust me anymore but that's all I said, except he wanted to know about Nathan and..." she looked at Joshua, "the homeless guy. Sorry, I didn't know your name. I knew nothing much, but he knows you're all working on something and I think he might cause trouble for you."

"Might! Do you know what he did to Lexi?" Zander demanded.

Patrice struggled to speak. "I'm so sorry, for everything. Tell me what I can do to help and after this is all over, can I see Lucy?"

Nathan looked serious. "Let's start with what you know about Ken Ferguson. And Lorna, I know you are working on a different tactic, but let's make sure you are up to speed on the bigger picture."

34

The Council meeting was full. Half the town was there, including many from the business community. The people who spoke didn't get a vote; they just gave the council members their viewpoint. Lexi worried that they would sway their opinion in favor rather than against. She also wondered how they all had information that the rest of the community didn't. This looked like a setup, a rag-tag bunch of nobodies against the great and the good. Lexi tried to remind herself that David beat Goliath. They just needed the right sized stone, and to know where to aim it.

The normal business of the meeting was settled quickly before the Chair rose to speak. "Tonight, we have a special motion that is not without controversy. May I first remind you; the city of Tribune has a right to sell surplus property or land in order to benefit the wider community. The property proposed to be sold was bought with money gifted to us by the late Ken Ferguson. When we agreed on the use of the land, we could not foresee that the city would undergo such growth. The money we can raise would not only pay to replace and move the current services but also used to provide even more services to the community and leave us with a healthy balance for new projects."

Lexi noticed that there was no mention of the Volt. She wasn't sure that everyone in the meeting was aware of what land he was referring to.

"We will take comments and questions later. First, I would like to call some of those who have been working tirelessly to make this opportunity available to Tribune. Mr. Fleming, would you like to begin?"

Frank sauntered towards the microphone. Lexi was in disbelief. He was shameless.

"Thank you for allowing me to share our vision of an improved Tribune. I believe in this town. It can be a wonderful place to live, to work and to bring up our families. I'm working to secure a deal with a billion-dollar company who loves what they see here. They want to bring jobs, new talent, and a new brighter future. We cannot disclose too many details yet, though as soon as we secure the land, we can close the deal and put Tribune on the map. I would ask you to put aside any rumors you may have heard and...."

A heckler from the back suddenly interrupted Frank. "It's not a rumor! You're selling the Volt to the highest bidder. You cannot silence us."

Lexi realized that the voice was from Victoria, the library clerk, and she was accompanied by her coworkers. The number of people had swelled and there were also residents from the Harbor. More shouts were heard.

"No gentrification."

"Save the Volt."

The Chair called the meeting to order and threatened to have anyone shouting thrown out. "I think we've heard what we need from Mr. Fleming for now, if you've written your name down to speak, we will begin calling you for your comments."

Frank looked at the protestors with bemusement. Lexi struggled to be silent. He was so confident, she hoped they had something to wipe the smile off his face.

"If you would just allow a few more minutes, we have a brief presentation." Frank looked across at Celeste, who nodded to someone at the back. As the lights were dimmed, a video appeared on the screen. A newly imagined version of Tribune. Children playing, happy smiling people riding bikes around paths that meandered through lush greenery. The images moved from fountains, lakes and flower gardens to tall glass and steel buildings housing busy professionals. A soft hypnotic voiceover promised a new Tribune where everyone would want to live. Celeste joined Frank and looked out at the crowd as if she was a mega-church preacher. "A new dawn awaits Tribune. Who has questions?"

The Chair looked annoyed that she appeared to be taking on his role. "Thank you. We will take questions in the same way we always do." He motioned Celeste to step down.

"Next we have the findings from an independently commissioned report from Underosa Communications. They have sent a representative from the company to read the highlights, the full report is available to read online."

A young woman, possibly an intern who Lexi had never seen before, read the prepared report. It presented a biased version of Lexi's findings, highlighting the cost savings and benefits while addressing none of the other concerns. For those not paying attention, it probably made a compelling argument. The NDA bound Lexi so she couldn't encourage the councilors to read the full report. By the time they did, it would probably be too late.

Lexi looked across at Amanda, who raised her eyebrows. She wondered if they were wasting their time. Hopefully, Amanda could pull something out of her hat.

A seemingly endless stream of locals and business people got up to have their say. Many were in favor of the project; they wanted the homeless away from the waterfront area. They didn't want their money "wasted" on more environmental projects.

Then it was Lorna's turn. Lexi was pleased that she'd agreed to come.

The Chairperson introduced her. "Dr. Greenleaf, I understand you will be speaking on behalf of the users of the Volt?"

Lorna stood behind the podium and began reading from prepared notes.

"I've only had the privilege of living in Tribune for a few years, yet in that time I've witnessed the life-changing services that the Volt offers. To you, it might be a place to check out a book, to have coffee, or buy fresh produce from the Eden. For others, it is community, a place to belong. Those new to the town quickly learn that the Volt will help them or point them in the right direction. Before the Harbor opened, we had women and children living in their cars after fleeing domestic violence. We also had many residents with mental health issues. Not everyone needs a therapist, sometimes they need a place to feel valued. That could be an exercise class, a warm shower, a kind word from the person making your coffee, a mentor listening to your business idea. The Volt has many services you probably aren't even aware of. Having it all under the same roof allows synergy between the different sections. Did you know that some of the new businesses that are thriving in town did not come directly from the entrepreneurial center, but first from the Harbor? I heard the disdain some of you expressed earlier. Many of those you malign were once successful business people themselves, just like you, and can be again, with our support. To scatter the services of the Volt will put an end to the wonderful work that has been done."

Lorna put aside her notes and took off her glasses. "The Volt is a vibrant community hub that has something for everyone. It is the envy of many of our neighboring towns. It would not be hyperbolic to claim that it not only enhances lives, it saves them. To send some of our most vulnerable residents to the other side of town would be a mistake based on no other motive than greed." Lorna gave a knowing smile to Lexi as she took her seat.

"Thank you, Doctor." "Next we have Amanda Lucas from the Eden"

Amanda leaned into the microphone and said, "Also Doctor."

The Chair was momentarily confused. "Doctor?"

"Doctor Amanda Lucas, it's on the card you have in front of you."

"Oh, I know you from the radio show. You're just Ask Amanda to me."

Lexi knew she would be less cool under the circumstances. She hoped Amanda had something to shut him up.

"I'm here in my official capacity as Dr. Amanda Lucas. The radio show I present, although somewhat educational, is mainly for entertainment purposes. Tonight, I want to speak to you as a scientist with a particular specialism in environmental science and endangered species."

The Chair slunk into his seat, and Amanda continued. "We are fortunate to live in an area of outstanding beauty, yet we also share it with many other species and some of them are threatened. Even more worrying, my research shows that we may have among us not one but two endangered species living in the area where the development is planned. We believe that the bayou is the site of endangered fresh-water mussels. Though I'm sure there is no construction planned yet, it would be fair to make sure that all the investors and potential developers know it would put any plans on hold until this can be investigated."

Frank rolled his eyes and threw a hand in the air, as if dismissing the idea.

"The project cannot go ahead if an endangered species is present. If there is evidence, then an environmental assessment will need to be done."

Deb played her part and asked the question in case no one else did. "You said two, what's the other species?"

"We believe that the big cat that has been seen is not a tiger, but possibly one of the rarest—the Florida Panther. If we can confirm that the Panther has made it all the way here, it would be one of only a tiny number left. We would do everything we could to preserve the habitat, which covers miles of green space around the Volt."

Lexi could see that Frank was taking this a little more seriously and wondered what Patrice thought of it all. She looked around but didn't see her. She realized she hadn't seen her since their earlier meeting.

Amanda concluded her speech and there were murmurs among the council members.

A few more people stood up to have their say and then the council planned to vote.

The chair and the council members convened, and returned only minutes later. "Ladies and gentlemen, it appears we need to do a little more research before we can make a decision. Amanda—sorry—Dr. Lucas, if you would share your findings with us, we will take the appropriate steps."

Lexi wanted to punch the air, but she knew she must maintain her cool. She caught sight of Patrice entering from the back of the room. It took a moment to realize that there were two police officers following her. They waited at the back until the meeting was officially over. As the meeting emptied, she slid into the seat next to Lexi, where the rest of the group joined her. Patrice said, "Wait a minute. Watch."

They had an unobstructed view of Frank. He appeared to be arguing with Celeste. He wasn't paying attention to the police officers who were walking towards him. One was readying his handcuffs.

"Mr. Fleming, we'd like to ask you a few questions. Come with us."

Frank recognized one of the officers. "Hey Tom, what's this about? Is this a joke?"

The other officer said, "Sir, you need to come with us. Do I need to use these?"

Frank grew more agitated and angrier. He was a man used to getting his way. He turned around and gestured towards the back of the room. "Let's go into the council chambers. We can talk better there, then you can tell me what this is all about."

The officer with the cuffs put them in front of Frank's face. "We need to talk to you about the hit-and-run death of Ken Ferguson. Last chance to do it the easy way."

Frank turned around to look for Celeste.

"I can't help you with this," she said. "I'll contact a defense lawyer."

Lexi looked at Patrice. "What just happened?"

"I've been naïve. I believed everything he told me. But once I learned what he tried to do to my cat and what he did to you Lexi, I realized he was capable of worse crimes. The night of Ken's death, he went out in a foul mood after we argued. When he came back, he was drunk. The next morning, I noticed damage to the car. He said he'd hit an animal, and it was my fault as I'd made him so mad. Later, when I heard about the hit and run, I convinced myself it was a coincidence. That was until he told me if anyone asked, I had to say he'd been at home with me. He claimed someone might try to pin it on him. And it was my car he was driving that night, he hinted that someone could believe I was driving, even convincing me he was *my* alibi. He didn't get the car fixed and kept it in the garage and then one day it was gone."

"Didn't anyone notice you'd stopped driving your car?" Deb couldn't imagine being without hers.

"I barely knew anyone. I was totally reliant on him."

Nathan said, "They might let him out if there isn't enough to hold him. You shouldn't go home tonight. I can get you somewhere safe. And talking of safe, I wonder where Matthew is? I've had my phone turned off. Let me see if there's been any message." Nathan checked his phone. "Nope still nothing."

Until now Lexi has struggled to muster up much concern for Matthew. Knowing the lengths Frank was prepared to go, she was less nonchalant. She hoped Matthew was safe.

Nathan looked around and saw they were almost the last people left in the council chambers. He led the group outside where the weather had turned cold. As they began to disperse, he said, "Hey you do all realize, tonight was only the opening gambit. Let's meet tomorrow morning at Tea."

35

———

Lᴇxɪ ᴡʜᴏ ᴡᴀs ɴᴏʀᴍᴀʟʟʏ ᴇᴀʀʟʏ, was surprised to find everyone already at Tea when she arrived. They had the place to themselves. Zander had brought a large cafetière of coffee to the big table, so he didn't have to keep getting up. Lexi poured herself a cup, deciding to forego her espresso. She didn't want to inconvenience Zander. "What did I miss?" she asked.

Nathan said, "We were just congratulating Amanda on a job well done. By the way, I heard from Matthew. He's on his way. Says he needs to speak to us."

Lexi silently took in the news about Matthew, she felt a huge sense of relief, yet she was still conflicted. She felt churlish but she'd had a lifetime to build up her resentment towards him, each time she broke down one wall another one seemed to appear in its place. "Amanda, what you did last night was amazing, but dare I ask, was it all true?"

Amanda said. "Lexi, you're a researcher. You know that I wouldn't tell lies and ruin my reputation. The mussels, yes, I have some good information from people I trust. An assessment will need to be done. The panther? Well, the good residents of Tribune believe they have seen one and I never claimed it to be a fact. I wanted to go with a Jaguarundi which is a much more exotic sounding cat and is small, unlike the much larger panther, but no one has seen one for decades. We'll probably get an avalanche of photos, more sightings and maybe some tracks or other evidence. It will bring out the crazies but might buy us some time. A company the size of Glass Jelly won't be put off, they have deep enough pockets and can afford surveys if they end up being required. Whereas I suspect Frank's investors might be less confident if they think there's a chance of losing their money."

Deb asked, "So just between us, do you think there really could be a panther, or a jagawatchamcallit? It would be a lot more interesting than a mussel. Who cares about mussels anyway?"

"Though I can neither confirm nor deny the existence of a local panther, I would caution you against writing off the humble mussel. They do a wonderful job of filtering the water in the bayou and removing bacteria and plankton. Without our meddling, they can live for decades."

"So why are they endangered?" Nathan asked.

"Many reasons, and I hate to say this as someone who loves fashion, vanity was part of the story. A couple of hundred years ago a German, John Boepple, came to the US. He began harvesting and crafting freshwater mussel shells into buttons. They were hugely popular and, like much in the natural world, there reaches a point where supply can't keep up with demand. So the mussel is not just a vehicle to save the Volt, if they find it to be in our waters I will fight for the little fellas. Oh, and you should know, in a twist of fate, Boepple stood on a mussel, cut his foot and died of blood poisoning."

Lexi frowned. "Sepsis. The same thing that killed my mom." She realized she'd brought the mood down but didn't feel like attempting to bring it back up.

They were all quiet for a moment. Zander rose from his seat and looked out towards the water. It was a beautiful fall day, and they all appeared bathed in a sunny glow. He turned back and sat. "I don't think I can stand to lose this place. But I can barely stay above water, and it's not just me, look...." Residents from the harbor were making their way through to the library, where an adult literacy session was about to begin. They would then come back to Tea and Two and enjoy a pastry and hot drink. "This place is special, we don't just meet physical needs we give people something to live for. From what you are saying Amanda, we could still fail?"

Amanda was about to answer when Matthew arrived, looking flustered. "I'm sorry I've been MIA, I'll explain later but something's happened. Joshua, your friend, he's in the hospital, He's in a bad way. Frank attacked him."

Patrice said, "No Frank's in Jail."

Matthew confirmed, "The arrest was on the news. He must have got bail late last night because he attacked Joshua in the early hours. Lexi, Nathan, he wants to see you, you need to come now. I have a rental car I can take you straight to him."

They both got up, and Lexi was still trying to figure it all out. "What were you doing at the hospital?"

"Come on, I'll tell you on the way." Matthew was impatient to get to the hospital and drove off as they were still buckling their seatbelts. "I'm sorry I worried you. The investment meeting had me freaked out, and I needed to do something rather than sit in my room and worry. I went to the hospital and asked if I could volunteer. They have lots of staff out with flu and are desperate, so they hired me to do locum work. They talked with the charity and fast tracked my background check. I worked the night shift and saw them bring..."

"Doc, stop! Wrong way!" Nathan screamed. Lexi hadn't noticed that as he was talking Matthew had taken a left turn towards the hospital and was driving on the wrong side of the road. A car was heading towards them. Nathan looked behind him, "You're clear! Move over, go!"

They were back on the right side of the road, leaving behind the honking of car horns. Matthew took a deep breath.

When Nathan had regained his composure he said, "Okay, focus on driving, let's get there in one piece. We can fill in the details when we see Joshua."

Lexi had only had a few seconds to process what had happened. "Trivia question, they drive on which side of the road in Kenya?"

"I'm sorry that hasn't happened before. I'm more focused when I'm driving on my own."

The front desk nurse recognized Matthew and let them go straight through to Joshua's room. Joshua was asleep but roused as he heard their voices. It surprised Lexi that he looked uninjured at first glance. He tried to get up, but the pain was too much. Matthew adjusted his pillows so he could raise his head enough to speak. "Joshua received a blow to the back of his head," Matthew explained. "He has some swelling. He was also kicked repeatedly while he was on the ground."

Joshua took a sip of water and then spoke slowly through his pain. "Someone woke me up knocking on the window of my van late last night. I thought it must be one of the guys out on the street though they rarely come so late. I couldn't see anyone so stepped outside and next thing I know I'm on the floor. He must have hit me with something heavy and knocked me out. As soon as I came around, he started kicking me. He wanted me to know it was him. He said I should have let the cat die, now I'd involved his wife he was taking it personally. He said to tell my new friends nothing was going to stop him."

He lifted his shirt and there was a chorus of gasps when they saw the evidence of Frank's brutality.

Lexi put her fist to her mouth to hold back her scream of rage. "The police, did you call them?"

"There are attacks on people living on the street every day. They're set on fire, urinated on, beaten, worse than this. I have no proof, and Frank and I have history. I don't have the energy, but I will go to the police if it will protect you. But first, I need you to do something. I have a safe deposit box; it has all my documents."

Joshua paused and lay back in the bed. He struggled to breathe, and it was a long minute before he continued. "There are also photographs, notes, a recording. It ties Frank to Ken's death. Matthew told me about the arrest, he'll have a good lawyer. They won't be able to prove it was him. Bring it back here and I'll talk you through what it all means."

Nathan took down the information. "Joshua, is there anything you need? Anyone we can contact?"

"I guess you'd better let my ex- and the kids know, just in case. I have to go back for a brain scan later, they're worried about the swelling."

Matthew said, "I can do that. Give me her number. If it's okay with you, I'll suggest they come to visit."

Lexi picked up something unsaid between them, and Joshua nodded.

"We'll let you get some rest." Matthew took the car keys from his pocket and Nathan put out his hands. "We've had enough drama for one day. I'll drive."

They arrived back at the Volt with the items from Joshua's safe deposit box. Amanda was waiting for them. "It's not good news guys, the mussel defense is unlikely to hold up, they could create the lake somewhere else. The panther idea was always a long shot, and even though Frank was arrested there are still people with money tied up who will turn a blind eye unless he's actually convicted of something."

Lexi wasn't ready to give up. "We might have other ways to stop him. This stuff from Joshua is all potential evidence. He's going to explain how we can use it, but we'll work through and see what is here before we go back to see him. We need to make notes. Nathan, you check the thumb drive." Lexi pulled out her notepad, and everyone smiled. She was back on form. "Zander, can we get some strong coffees over here, we need to focus."

Matthew took back the car keys from Nathan. "I'm going to get back to the hospital. I don't want to be paranoid, but if Frank's getting desperate, Joshua might not be safe. I also want to see if the police have interviewed him."

"Matthew, take this and stick it on your dashboard." Lexi handed Matthew a handwritten note. It read,

DRIVE ON THE RIGHT!!

"Okay, you got me." Matthew chuckled. "When you've worked through the information, message me. If Joshua is up to it, we can see what he has to tell us."

Lexi studied the journals, and Nathan checked the photographs on a thumb drive. Amanda continued to search for anything useful among the other bits and pieces that were in the box.

"You know, even if we can prove Frank is corrupt or has committed a crime, it doesn't mean someone else can't take the lead on the project. He and Celeste Collins seem pretty tight. She's probably in a lot deeper than she's letting on."

"What are you saying Amanda?" Lexi asked. "That this is all pointless?" Lexi put down her pen and pushed her fingers up through her hair.

"No, keep searching. We need proof that Frank knew with Ken off the scene, he would have a clear run at getting his hands on the Volt."

"That would mean he was playing a long game though?" Nathan pointed out.

Amanda sighed, "Do you think this is the first chance he's had? He might have tried before, or this could be the big deal he's been waiting for. If he's going to make millions, it would be worth the wait, and he may not have planned to kill Ken. Just saw the opportunity. Though of course the police don't seem to have anything to hold him. That's why we have to keep looking."

Patrice arrived with Deb. "Frank called me; he's pretending that everything's normal. I guess he can't afford to throw my stuff on the street and draw more attention to himself. He claimed that it was all a misunderstanding. Thanks, Nathan, for finding me the place to stay. What can I do to help?" She made a point of sitting next to Deb, Lexi could see a thaw between them.

Deb smiled. "This reminds me of books I read as a kid where they solve a mystery."

Nathan grimaced, "This has moved into an 'attempted murder' mystery."

Lexi updated them and looked to her notes. "Can I clarify what we have and work out a timeline? I'm getting a little bogged down in details here. Patrice, you should be able to help with this. This is what I have from Joshua's journal. The meeting where Ken offered to donate the money to build the Volt was September 4. That is also in the minutes of the meeting. I then have a note that a week later, Ken met with the Council Finance Committee. He gave them a check, they agreed to draw up a document earmarking the money to be used for the specific purpose intended. They would take it to the next council meeting for approval. I've no record that ever happened, and that is why they claim they could go ahead. Why didn't it happen though?"

Patrice thought for a moment. "I bet I know why, this was four years ago right, there was a hurricane around that time, it was my first one, so I remember. It wasn't particularly bad, though it did some damage to downtown buildings. If you check the records, you'll probably find it was rescheduled."

Nathan looked up the council website that included online meeting minutes. "Lexi, add this to your timeline. They rescheduled the October meeting to November."

Lexi said, "Ken was killed in the hit and run at the end of October. Joshua began following Frank soon after that. He saw him try to drown Lucky around a week later. A few days after that, Joshua confronted Frank. Less than a week later, Joshua was attacked and thrown in the river."

Deb looked confused. "Why exactly was Joshua following Frank? Have I missed a step?"

Amanda agreed, "It's not just you, there is something else. I think it's time to go see Joshua. But before you do, Patrice, didn't anyone question Frank at the time of Ken's death? Were there any other suspects? What did you tell the police to make them question him this time?"

"There was no reason to suspect Frank, nothing to tie him to it. I don't know where he was that night but likely somewhere shady. No one saw anything."

Amanda asked, "Aren't you worried he could say it was you? It could be a case of 'he said, she said.'"

Patrice paused. "I don't want this leaving this room, for now anyway. We know what Frank is capable of. He doesn't know, but I have an alibi... that night was the first time he'd been aggressive enough to make me scared that one day he would hurt me. I've always told myself he's never hit me, but it's not strictly true. That night he pushed me hard and I fell. I wasn't hurt, but I was shaken that he would do that to me. I sat outside and cried. The woman who lives opposite must have heard me.

She came over, told me she was there if I needed her. I never told Frank, he says she's a busybody. I've talked to her a bit since I've lived there, and I went to see her this week. She remembers that night, she made notes when she heard arguments. She volunteers for a domestic abuse helpline and says people always forget to record things, so she did it for me. She's given a statement. I'd also taken photographs of my damaged car."

Deb gave her a high five that landed awkwardly. "Whoa! remind me not to mess with you."

Everyone continued working quietly until Nathan broke the silence. "Hey, look at this photo. Isn't that Ken Ferguson with Joshua?" The photo showed Ken with his arm around Joshua's shoulder.

Amanda confirmed, "I remember that event. It was a fundraising dinner. Ken donated to a lot of charities. Joshua often worked freelance and covered stories for the Trib, among others."

"They look more than just acquaintances," Lexi noted. "He looked happy. Guess this was before he had the misfortune of crossing Frank."

Nathan's phone pinged with a message. "Matthew's on his way back he said to wait here. Maybe he has what he needs from Joshua and is leaving him to rest?"

Lexi suggested, "Let's keep looking. There is likely more to find. I will make notes of anything we come up with."

Matthew arrived back twenty minutes later. He slumped into a chair. After a long silence, he spoke. "Joshua, he didn't make it."

Nathan stood up, "Then it's murder."

Lexi felt suddenly desperate, guilty, responsible, had she brought this about by involving Joshua? She opened her mouth to speak and paused, then she asked. "Matthew, you knew

Joshua might die, didn't you? You encouraged him to see his family. But he looked fine, he was in pain, but he was talking."

"I hoped I was wrong. He wasn't in good health to begin with and had some liver damage. We were concerned with the swelling to his brain, but the internal injuries to his abdomen were also severe. We couldn't stop the bleeding."

No one knew what to say. Patrice looked like she might throw up. Deb looked bewildered. Amanda motioned Matthew to sit back down, "Tell us what happened."

"We talked, he told me more about Frank. The police came, but they didn't have any evidence to tie it to Frank. They say there have been other attacks on members of the homeless community. They are looking at his attack as part of a wider investigation. They don't believe Frank would have immediately gone to attack Joshua after being released from custody."

Amanda sighed. "He thinks he's untouchable, killing Joshua was just tying up loose ends. We can't let him get away with this."

Matthew barely knew Joshua, but he was visibly devastated.

Amanda spoke again, "The best thing we can do to honor Joshua is to get him justice. He told us there were answers here, let's find them, let's nail Frank. Matthew, was he able to tell you anything else before he died?"

"He said there are photos of the cat, that he and Ken were friends and Celeste—that she knows something."

Lexi said, "You carry on here. I'm going to find Celeste, I have a plan."

36

Lexi hadn't driven since the incident with Frank. She hoped
this trip would end better. She knew Celeste had a downtown
office and started her hunt there. Celeste prided herself on
being the alpha female of the town. She was on all the right
committees, only associated with those who could further her
goals, and would not let anyone get in her way. Lexi suspected
that the Volt deal might even be her idea. Lexi wasn't scared of
her. It felt different than dealing with Frank, but Lexi didn't
know what to expect and didn't want to underestimate Celeste.
Though Lexi had said she had a plan, she barely had half of one
and hoped it would unfold if she could get Celeste to open up.
She'd done a little research on Celeste's business and hadn't
found much. The lawyer didn't appear to have been involved in
many high-profile cases. She found a Glass Jelly page that
focused on her charity work, but Lexi wondered if Celeste's
public profile was a lot of smoke and mirrors

Lexi parked behind the building where Celeste's office was
located. The photograph on the website made it appear that she
used the whole place. That might have been the case once, but it
was clear that she was now sharing the space with other

businesses, including a chiropractor and a maid service. The building was faded from years in the sun and it needed a coat of paint.

Before Lexi entered the building, she made a call. She hoped she wouldn't need the cavalry, but if she did, it would be wise to have them on standby. She steeled herself for the confrontation, made her way to Celeste's office and knocked on the door.

Lexi heard the sound of multiple locks being turned and was surprised to see Celeste appear at the door. She'd expected a receptionist or assistant.

"Oh, it's you. Well, do come in."

Lexi hoped Celeste would drop the fake southern hospitality. She had one of those butter-wouldn't-melt smiles and an accent and demeanor that made Lexi wonder if she'd watched *Gone with the Wind* too many times.

"What can I do for you Alexandra? Oh, yes, I know all about you."

"Do you also know that Frank is implicated in another murder? He was barely out of jail before he attacked someone else who got in his way. Joshua died as a result of his injuries."

Celeste seemed genuine in her assertion that she knew nothing about Joshua. "Frank has some unorthodox business methods, but I doubt he would resort to violence."

"You know he attacked me, right?"

"He said he talked to you, that's all."

"Celeste, you may believe that the end justifies the means, but I have a team of investigators looking into everything to do with the Volt deal. Frank may well have got away with one murder, but you are hedging your bets if you're comfortable being tied to him when there are now two."

"I have nothing to do with Frank's methods. We might both

be involved in the same business deal, but that doesn't make me responsible for everything he does."

"Are you sure about that? Would the kidnapping of a cat make you any more involved?"

Celeste was silent for a moment. "I heard something about that, but didn't it happen while we were all at the race. You must have seen me there. I mean half the world have seen the video that was uploaded to Glass Jelly."

"I saw you arrive late, you still had time to sneak into my apartment. Do you know anything about DNA Celeste? We humans leave it everywhere, when you have long, shiny hair like yours it's easy to find. My apartment's always pristine. Anything out of place is very noticeable. *Top Lawyer Accused of Cat Napping and Harassment* would be a great headline. It would make fascinating reading in the local paper, it might even reach the nationals, especially if they include that you also illegally entered an apartment owned by *The Girl with the Body*. I've heard *Fly Guy Private Eye*, is working on the story right now. So why don't you tell me something I might find useful."

Lexi wondered if Celeste was considering her next move. She was hard to read, her micro-expressions were masked by the paralyzing effects of her facial treatments. Lexi was playing a role. She didn't know how long she could keep it up, so she gambled and continued.

"Celeste, you know the value of the Volt's location. You sit on boards and volunteer on committees. I'm guessing they're goldmines for information. The beauty of this plan is that your hands will be clean if anything goes wrong. If it all comes back to bite the developers. You'll still walk away with a profit. How much was your investment?"

Celeste smirked. Lexi wondered if, as an aspirational pacifist, she should be thinking what an extremely punchable face Celeste had.

"There is, of course, the possibility that the town won't get the contract with the major player we are wooing. Even if they don't, we've set in motion something that will be difficult to overturn. Do you think I play along with the mayor's fundraisers and wear a damned tutu for fun?"

"So," Lexi asked, "if it all came to nothing and they implicate you in Frank's crimes, how long do you think you would still practice law and be invited on boards and committees?"

"Oh, come on, I relocated a cat, no one's going to care about that."

"So, you admit it? You broke into two private homes and caused criminal damage. If you did that at Frank's behest, what else would you do? What size shoes do you wear Celeste? The boot marks on Joshua's abdomen were quite distinctive."

"I had nothing to do with that. And you have nothing on me."

"It's murder Celeste, I hope you have a good alibi." Lexi thought she saw the tiniest shift in Celeste's coolness, then they heard a man's voice.

"Is this fruit loop bothering you?"

Celeste jumped back and Lexi saw she was afraid of Frank, who'd been listening to their conversation.

"So, he's dead. Good. Now, I only have to deal with you."

Lexi wasn't afraid. She was furious, as she had been since he'd attacked her. "Glass Jelly won't want to work with you when they know what you've been up to. No one will."

"So you know about them. What else might you have learned by breaking into a prominent lawyer's office?"

Frank opened the filing cabinet and began throwing files around.

Celeste grabbed his arm. "What are you doing? Are you crazy?"

He shrugged her off. "This is the story. She came in here while you were in the restroom and began searching through your files. I caught her, now you need to call the police. We need her out of the way." Frank pushed papers into Lexi's hands. "DNA you said right? Yes, I heard you. Yours is going to be all over here by the time I'm finished making my citizen's arrest. He shoved Lexi hard. She fell, her head glancing across the corner of Celeste's desk.

Damn, that hurt.

"Frank, no! This has gone too far." Celeste seemed unsure of what to do.

Frank grabbed his phone and dialed. "Police please. Yes, I'm at the Law Office of Celeste Collins in downtown Tribune, she's encountered a violent intruder and is a little shaken up. Can you come straight away? I had to use reasonable force. The intruder might need an ambulance."

Lexi held a hand to her head, and it came away bloody. But she was determined Frank wasn't going to beat her. She dragged herself to her knees and grabbed a glass object from the desk. It was heavy and unwieldy, and Frank, who was still on the phone, never saw it coming.

The leaded glass crashed into Frank's leg. He screamed in pain, then yelled a disappointedly predictable, "You little bitch, I'll kill you!"

Celeste retrieved the object. "That's my businesswoman of the year award, thank you. Frank, you'd better not do her any more damage if the police are on the way. And you know I don't approve of violence. It's so unnecessary."

Frank rubbed his leg and hobbled towards the exit. "I'm going out to meet them. Keep an eye on her."

Lexi didn't like the look of all the blood staining Celeste's carpet. She hoped her wound felt worse than it was. Maybe it would give Celeste cause to worry about her part in it. Lexi didn't know how far Celeste was prepared to go with Frank's schemes, but banked on her caring about her reputation. "Celeste, think about what you're doing. You don't want to be involved in any of this. One call from me and all the other stuff goes away. It's Frank who's the bad guy here. You can see he's lost it. If you go along with this you are on the hook for everything else he's done."

Celeste looked out the window to where Frank probably waited, "You really think I care about the cat burglary stuff? I can discredit any evidence you have. I'm a damn good lawyer."

Lexi grabbed the box of tissues from the desk and pressed a wad of them to her aching head. It probably looked gruesome. "Celeste, what do you think Frank is going to do? Kill everyone who gets in his way? Eventually it will catch up with him, and with you. Have you ever been in prison? Imagine what your hair will look like after a few months without your stylist." An appeal to her vanity was the last attempt at getting Celeste to see sense, yet it seemed to have got her thinking.

"What do you expect me to do? The police are on their way. It's our word against yours."

"They aren't idiots. He's been out of jail less than a day and people around him are getting injured, dying. I came here because we have evidence linking you to Ken Ferguson, your name was on a dying man's lips and my team are currently working through his evidence. There's probably more linking you to a motive for Ken's death than there is to Frank."

Lexi had no idea what evidence there actually was but it seemed to have Celeste rattled.

"What do you want me to do?"

Lexi dragged herself to her feet and looked around the room. "Is there a back way out of this building?"

"I'll help you if you say I didn't have anything to do with

this. Frank can fix his own mess." Celeste pushed Lexi towards a door in a kitchen area that led out into the parking lot.

Lexi handed Celeste her car keys. "I can't see to drive with all this blood in my eyes. Drive me back to the Volt."

"You might need the hospital."

"There's a doctor there."

While Celeste drove, Lexi made the call she'd hoped she could avoid.

"Remi, I should have listened to you. Did you find anything?" She swallowed. "I'm going to need that lawyer."

The voice from the phone asked. "Let me see you?"

"No."

"Lexi, I need to see you're okay."

Lexi turned on her video. The blood had started to clot but, her eyes were blackening, and she looked like she'd been in a fight.

"What the hell happened?"

Lexi gave Remi the short version. "I'm coming, I will be there in a few hours. I told you I would be there if you need me, and you need me right now."

Lexi tried to stop him; "You can't spoil the tour. People rely on you."

"Lexi, I'm in Mexico making a dumb video. We don't even start for a couple of days. Send me your location. I'm on it."

Lexi sent him the details with a message.

Remember, this is a small town. Do you remember how to do low key?

Celeste had been listening with intrigue. "Please tell me that was *the* Remi Lal and he's coming on a private jet. You're full of surprises."

"You know who he is?"

"I have a teenage daughter. He's hard to avoid."

When they arrived at the Volt, the shock of seeing Lexi's injuries was only matched by the fact that she was accompanied by Celeste. Matthew went into full doctor mode. Once he'd cleaned her wound, he confirmed it probably wasn't so bad. "You really should get it checked out and you need a stitch or two. I could drive you to the hospital,"

"I might be about to be arrested, and we have some work to do. Can't you fix it for me?"

Matthew looked around. "Does anyone have a sewing kit?"

Zander went behind the counter and returned with a needle and thread, hot water and a small glass of dark liquid. "You need to sterilize it, and Lexi, you might need the brandy. This is going to hurt, right Doc?"

"Thank you, Dr. Zander, I'm sure Matthew is familiar with hygiene protocols." Lexi mock scowled at him and reached for the drink. She knocked it back in one gulp.

Deb watched in awe as Matthew expertly stitched Lexi's forehead. "Will it scar?" she asked.

Matthew tied the final suture and cut the remaining thread. "I've had over twenty years to perfect my invisible mending skills. I can stitch the face of a baby, and no one would know there had been an injury, unless they knew where to look."

Celeste had been quiet while Lexi was taken care of. "Look, I knew Frank was ruthless in business but I didn't know he was capable of this. I'll tell the police you did nothing, but you, you all have to tell them I wasn't part of his other stuff. I care about this town, yes. I want to make money, but I don't want to hurt people. The deal would have eventually been good for everyone."

Lexi demanded another brandy after the first jab of the needle. She wasn't a big drinker and its effects were kicking in.

"If you stick around, you can help us make sure he... Oh crap, I think I had a plan but now it's gone."

Lexi's phone pinged. It was Remi.

I'm almost there. Where's the nearest helipad?

Lexi rolled her eyes and typed,

I said LOW KEY! Remember!

Just kidding!

Amanda and Nathan had gone back to huddling over their laptops. Now the focus was off Lexi, Amanda was ready with an update. "Celeste, you claim to want to help, so tell us what you know about Ken Ferguson and the money that was earmarked for the Volt?"

Celeste flinched as if someone had slapped her. "What, I— there was never an official agreement, we talked about it but never."

Amanda placed a sheaf of papers in front of Celeste. "This is a printout of a document that you drew up for Ken Ferguson. It was a letter that should have accompanied the donation, but Ken was naïve, he trusted you, he agreed to allow them to have the money in advance to start the project. It would have created a permanent restriction. The Volt was supposed to become a non-profit. Ken trusted you," she repeated. "Why did you betray him?"

"The council decided to do things differently."

Amanda said. "I'm not a lawyer but it seemed that you had written confirmation of Ken's wishes. He paid you to do a job and you kept it quiet for your own ends. That is a conflict of interest."

The group was digesting the information and any positive feelings they'd had towards Celeste were fast evaporating.

Zander could see that Lexi was fading. "Hey, what can I get you?"

Lexi put her head on the table. "I need to lie down; I'm going to curl up in one of the booths for a while."

Matthew said. "You shouldn't go to sleep; you probably have a concussion. I'm heading back to the hospital, why not come with me and get checked out?"

She shook her head. "I need to be here. There's a rock star flying in from Mexico."

37

Remi was dressed simply in jeans and a graphic t-shirt, yet none of this could erase his perfectly groomed beauty. He rushed to Lexi, shaken to see her bruises and the stitched cut that was now accompanied by a swelling the size of an egg. "What has he done to you? You made me bring a lawyer. This is Sandi, by the way. I should have brought a doctor, or a boxer, to do the same to him."

"I've already seen a doctor." Lexi made the introductions, and Sandi, the lawyer joined Amanda and Nathan.

No one but Zander had any idea what was happening, he gave the group the edited highlights of how Lexi and Remi were connected.

When things calmed down, Remi talked privately to Lexi. "You know, once people know I'm here, there's a chance the story will come out about how we know each other. I'm used to it, they know everything about me, but you? Are you ready for it? I can make up a story that doesn't involve you."

Lexi smiled. "It's time to stop hiding from who I am."

Remi gave her a gentle hug, then said, "I've had a couple of hours to talk to Sandi about Tribune's troubles. Give her some time with your friends. She's creative at finding loopholes. If she wasn't I'd still be doing commercials for some awful products I agreed to before I knew better."

Lexi was feeling a tiny sliver of hope when, out of her peripheral vision, she saw blue flashing lights. She could barely gain the group's attention before two police officers came through the main doors to the Volt.

"Lexi Weaver, you need to come with us to answer some questions."

Nathan jumped up. "She's done nothing wrong. Frank Fleming attacked her. Ask her." He pointed to the now empty chair where Celeste had been sitting. She was gone.

Sandi leaned in and quietly said to Remi, "I'm not a criminal lawyer, but I think I can handle this." Turning to the police, she said, "My client will be happy to answer your questions. I will bring her to you myself."

Remi looked panicked. "I'll call the driver. I'm coming with you."

"No Remi," Sandi said, "you need to stay out of sight. You might make things worse. Guys is it possible to close this place down for a while? Who's in charge? We'll compensate you."

Zander stood and readied to close the shutters to the other parts of the Volt. "No problem. I'll close the blinds too."

Remi joined Amanda and Nathan. "I have an idea that could help you. Can you answer me some questions and then give me a little time to make some calls? Let's see what we can do to give Lexi some good news."

Remi finished speaking. He looked at Lexi and he touched just below his eyebrow with his index finger, to others it meant nothing, Lexi knew in their childhood language it meant "Sister."

38

LEXI'S ANXIETY WAS RISING. What if they put her in a cell? She couldn't handle it, the dirt, the smell. They kept her hanging around for hours and no one communicated with her. When a detective finally questioned her, it wasn't what she was expecting. They wanted answers about Frank, her side of the story of the events at Celeste's office, what she knew about Joshua, even Frank's previous threats to her. She couldn't figure out if they believed her. Sandi made sure she said nothing to implicate herself. The cut on her forehead looked gruesome, even with Matthew's perfect stitching, and her blackened eyes made her look as if she'd taken a beating. The detective looked almost sympathetic. Then suddenly, without explanation, she was free to go. As they left the police station, she saw Celeste. What was she doing there?

Remi's driver took them, not to the Volt as she expected, but to the Grand Hotel. Remi had obtained a suite, and everyone was there when they arrived.

Lexi was surprised to see that everyone seemed upbeat. "Have you all been drinking while I've been in jail?"

Remi was still upset at Lexi's appearance, he put his arm

around her shoulder and led her to join everyone on the suite's huge wraparound sofa. "We've been working our butts off and are celebrating what we hope is a win."

Lexi looked at them all curiously.

Sandi said. "I gave Remi some suggestions of how he could help you to fight city hall." She looked at Remi. "Though please tell me you've not actually signed anything without your lawyer present?"

Remi asked, "Amanda, will you explain what we've been working on? You have the storytelling radio voice."

Lexi looked at Remi and down at her clothes that still had blood on them, "I need to get cleaned up. I can't bear to wear these clothes for another minute."

"There's a robe in the bathroom and Patrice brought you some clothes from the gift shop, they might not be to your taste, but they're clean."

Lexi was grateful that Remi knew her well enough to have thought ahead. "Thanks, and thank you Patrice. Give me ten minutes."

Patrice smiled. "For some reason Remi thought it might cause a stir to be seen shopping at a hotel gift shop for women's loungewear."

Deb laughed as Zander checked if everyone was good for drinks. "Relax Zander, you're not our butler, though this fancy suite has one if we want it. 'Premium services available' it says here." She tapped the amenities card.

Lexi returned wearing the hotel branded clothing. "Shame they don't have a premium clothing line."

Amanda allowed Lexi to be seated and then began. "Everyone, pay attention. There's a lot to take in. We know that Frank was behind the plan to gain ownership of the Volt and surrounding land with the money from the investors. He thought he was on the verge of signing a deal with Glass Jelly.

Frank used Glass Jelly's name as the carrot to get people to invest. Coincidentally, Glass Jelly is sponsoring Remi's upcoming tour." Remi took a seated bow. "The company has divested from anything that damages the environment, and were horrified to hear that Frank was prepared to bulldoze, yes literally, an area that might be home to an endangered species."

Lexi was struggling, she closed her eyes, clearly still in some discomfort. Nathan leaned towards her and spoke gently, "Lexi, this is good news, stay with us."

Amanda continued, "It surprised Glass Jelly that Remi knew about the deal, as Frank, who loves making everyone else sign binding agreements seemed to have forgotten he signed one himself. He wasn't supposed to disclose that he was even in discussions with them. He faces a massive penalty for doing so."

"And how does this save the Volt?" Lexi asked.

"Let me tell her this bit," Remi said. "Glass Jelly has been wanting me to accept a bigger sponsorship deal, but they have concerns over how much I travel. They want to find a way for us to make it work. They won't sue Frank if he removes himself from any deals and agrees never to have anything to do with the future of the Volt. He can't even set foot in it, and he has to make a public statement."

Nathan reminded them. "And he's still being investigated for two murders which Remi is going to hire investigators for. They may be able to make sense of the evidence we have."

"Okay, so back to the Volt. Amanda has been talking to Glass Jelly's Environmental Wizard, Tzar, or whatever she's called. Glass Jelly needs to prove their green creds." Remi said.

Amanda looked disapprovingly at Remi. "Hey Mr. Jet Set, their *Earth Impact Officer* doesn't merely want to *prove* their green credentials, this isn't about greenwashing. They are committed to making a difference and they want to offset their environmental impacts, like people they sponsor flying on private jets."

Lexi's head was throbbing, "You two, can you stop with the pissing contest, where is this going?"

Zander was beaming, "Lexi, they are going to fund the Volt."

Amanda clarified. "They were looking for somewhere to focus their environmental work before they'd even heard of Tribune. Their new campus was supposed to showcase it. They've already committed to use sustainable resources, solar, geothermal heat pumps, compostable toilets it was all in the plans. Frank and his people only focused on the money to be made. Glass Jelly didn't want to destroy the town. They didn't know Frank was trying to sell it to them purely for profit."

"So, are you saying they are still going to build here?" Lexi asked

"Instead of buying an empty plot, they're going to work with us. And they are going to hire me to work for them *and* fund the Eden. They're excited about the fresh water mussels. It's exactly the type of educational project they like to work on. The campus might come here at a later date, in a different location but right now they want to begin the partnership. Working with grass-roots organizations is what they do. If Frank and Celeste had done their due diligence instead of only looking at dollars signs, they might have seen that Glass Jelly would never have signed a deal with them."

Deb had switched off but tried to catch up. "Hang on, I thought we didn't have mussels, you made them up."

Amanda laughed. "No, you made the panther up. There are mussels—well, there were, if Frank hasn't tried to destroy them already."

Patrice had been quiet. She had a sorrowful air of guilt around her, but she had a question. "Wasn't the city selling the land in order to make a huge profit. Are Glass Jelly paying them?"

It was Nathan's turn. "It took Sandi about five minutes to figure out they couldn't sell something that they didn't really own. There's paperwork proving there was an agreement to earmark the money for the Volt. Ken died believing he had given a gift to Tribune. Celeste sat on it, but it's all here. Sandi reckons we have enough to make a case, or at least stop them from selling it to anyone else. Glass Jelly has agreed to fund new services. They will eventually take it out of council control and run it as a non-profit. If those on the council who were in league with Frank want to keep their jobs and reputation, they need to play nice."

Lexi looked at Remi. "You really made good on your promise. It looks like you've saved us. Though this all sounds too good to be true."

Remi looked at Lexi's swollen and bruised face. "Without you, my life would have been very different. You all know she saved me right? I was a frightened child who didn't want to live, and because of Lexi, I and an army of others, help kids who are bullied like I once was. This is a case of perfect timing. Glass Jelly has been trying to get me to work with them for a while. Doing it now means I can pull in favors, though I believe they genuinely do want to work with Tribune."

Matthew was trying to piece it all together. "So, they don't want to build the campus here? I was in the investors' meeting. The plans seemed pretty firm. Oh no, should I have said that? I was undercover."

Sandi laughed. "You went in good faith... well, kind of. No one will care. Those plans, the video, they were generic to lure the investors. Glass Jelly had nothing to do with them." She added, "I want to be clear about something. Yes, Lexi is fortunate in having a friend like Remi with all the resources he can command, yet you all did an amazing job in your own right. Dr. West you took a risk going undercover. Discovering that Glass Jelly was Frank's potential client was a key component. And your friend who passed, he has been onto this Frank for a long time. The users of the Volt and this town, owe you all a debt of gratitude."

Matthew said. "I'm relieved to hear that and, as a doctor, may I prescribe some rest for everyone. This has been a hell of an exhausting day."

Nathan agreed. "Let's reconvene tomorrow at the Volt. We still have some work to do before we can relax."

Remi shook his head. "I think you're all going to have to avoid the Volt tomorrow there's a rumor going around that someone famous has been hanging out there."

Everyone looked at their phones to see the latest Glass Jelly posts.

"Let's meet back here in the morning." Lexi grinned. "Remi, breakfast is on you."

39

REMI HAD INSISTED that Lexi stay at the hotel. She went downstairs early in the morning to see if the shops in the lobby had anything more suitable for her to wear. She wasn't surprised to find the hotel teeming with reporters. Sandi had arranged for security guards to be posted on the floor where Remi was staying. As the group arrived, they enjoyed being treated like VIPs. They helped themselves to a lavish breakfast.

Nathan tapped the table lightly. "First, can I confirm, everyone is safe, no one is in jail, and we can account for all cats. Great! Get comfortable."

Lexi said. "Zander's on his way. Tea and Two had a line outside the door. He's brought in some extra help; he's getting them set up. Though they might have to close early, they won't have enough food."

Amanda nodded her head, "I've been getting calls all morning, the rumors are crazy, someone saw us all together, they think Remi's in town to do a charity fundraiser."

Remi smiled, "Not a bad idea."

Nathan asked, "Any quick updates before I begin?"

"Well, a lying, murderous husband is in jail," Patrice said as she fought back tears of joy. "I've traded him in for a cat—she remembers me by the way, even after all this time."

Lexi asked, "You went home? What about Frank?"

Nathan confirmed, "Patrice is back in her home. We had her locks changed early this morning. Frank has been re-arrested; he's unlikely to get bail. Sandi and I did more work last night. We transcribed recordings and deciphered journals. The photographs and video of Frank attempting to drown the cat were compelling, they were time-stamped. The police are seeing a picture of a violent man who lies. We might not be able to get justice for Ken Ferguson, we haven't found anything new there, but hopefully we can for Joshua. A witness has come forward who saw Frank attack him. And best of all, Celeste has made a statement confirming that he attacked you, Lexi."

Surprised, Lexi asked, "What will happen to Celeste?"

Sandi answered, "You all agreed not to mention her kidnapping, catnapping, whatever, and I'm still trying to figure out why that was necessary or why she'd agree to it. She could face some trouble for sitting on the information about Ken's donation. It will certainly tarnish her professional reputation in this town. Though from what we've uncovered about her, she seems to have been having financial issues, it's possible that's why she went along with Frank's plans."

Nathan asked. "How did we discover she was the cat napper, by the way? I checked out the area we recognized. Remember from the reflection in Bella's eyes? The only connection with the area was you, Zander."

Zander took a double take. "You think I'm a cat napper? I'm sorry I'm uncomfortable with that term. It sounds like someone who sleeps at the office during meetings. You think I kidnapped a cat?"

Suddenly, everyone was laughing at the absurdity of the situation. Nathan explained, "No, of course not, but I was looking for someone familiar and you live there. I didn't know that Celeste also has a rental home."

Lexi said, "Just call me Inspector Weaver. She left her hair all over my place. Okay, she left at least three of her long hairs in my apartment. I notice things like that."

Sandi, used to dealing with multimillion dollar contracts, said, "This is a strange little town. Do small town gangsters deal in cats rather than horse's heads? I'm still not getting it."

Patrice said, "Frank does things because he can. In his mind, it sent a message that he knew Lexi and Deb were connected. He's paranoid. He also probably had some hold over Celeste. It was another power play."

Nathan added, "Frank should be paranoid, he has his fingers in a lot of pies. Deb you remember the envelope you opened with the fake id's? Looks like he's been doing favors for some very shady people in town. Don't worry, there's no connection to you, though all his dealings are going to come out. I hear *Fly Guy Private Eye's* Column is moving to the front page for next week's edition of the paper." Nathan addressed Deb, "I know this is awkward, but have you told the police that Frank is blackmailing you. I'm sorry I realized I never followed up on DNA on the envelope with all that's been happening?"

Deb looked to her feet. "No, because he's not. And thanks Nathan for outing me! You may as well all know I received some revealing photos in the mail. Y'all know I'm not a saint. I thought it was Frank because, well he'd threatened me enough times and he'd done something similar to Joshua."

Nathan pulled a face. "Oops, sorry I thought everyone knew, so how do you know it wasn't Frank?"

"It was the guy, the one-night stand guy, well, him and his wife. It's their thing, they get off on it, she stays out for the night, he records what he gets up to. That's why he was so keen to get me out of there so she could come back, and they could both watch the video. Sick right?"

Lexi screwed up her face, "So why did he send the photographs?"

"Because—oh you won't believe this—he works at the library. He's seen me there a lot recently. I never noticed him, I barely remembered what he looked like. He thought I was following him, and I was going to say something to his boss. They just think he's a happily married boring library clerk. I saw him making a door sign for a meeting room wall, it had the same bold handwriting as the envelope with the photographs, that's when I thought he looked familiar. Before you say it, I know. I'm dealing with him. He's a moron, nice body though."

Amanda asked, "So is the Volt safe?"

Sandi was one of those people who liked to pace around the room when she talked. She had an air of authority, and everyone was glad she was on their side. She answered, "I came here as a favor to Remi. I'm not his personal lawyer, if you were wondering. I work for his recording company, but he is our biggest asset, and we like to keep him happy. It was a fortunate coincidence that Glass Jelly was in the picture. They had no official agreement with Frank or this town, but now they've found people on the ground they can trust. There might be a role for each of you, if you want it. Amanda, as you know, is already onboard."

Zander had arrived and had been bursting to ask. "What about Tea and Two?"

Remi signaled for Sandi to sit. "Let me take this one, Sandi. You can be a little harsh and we are talking about this guy's dream."

Sandi sat and pretended to look offended.

"Zander, before we can even talk about the future of your business, I would need to know your intentions?"

"My?"

"Intentions, with my sister. Do you intend to..."

Lexi picked up a bread roll and threw it at Remi's head. "Remi, behave!"

Remi continued," Okay, I'm playing with you, though I think you should both go on a date. Now to Tea and Two, let's be honest, it's not really working, is it?"

There was an audible gasp in the room.

"No, don't misunderstand me, the Volt needs it. I understand that everyone loves Tea and Two, but it still has to make money and it needs a rebrand. If you are willing to accept help, then Glass Jelly will work with you or rather they will pay someone. How about you Patrice?'

"I plan to divorce Frank."

"That's good, but I was asking about the rest of your life. Would you work with Zander? You could transform the place. That's your thing, right? You could redesign it to appeal to readers who like more, well, contemporary literature. Or you could consider turning it into a cat cafe, they are huge in many of the markets we work in."

Lexi had forgotten that Remi had such a wicked sense of humor.

"Don't you dare!"

Patrice looked thoughtful. "I loved design and I'm not saying I wouldn't help, but there are some bigger issues I need to look at. You all recognized I was being manipulated, abused. I couldn't see it. If I hadn't met you, or if Frank wasn't in jail, I might be still with him, living in denial while things escalated. I need to help women like me."

Sandi answered, "This is all new, we have time. There will be lots of plans and meetings to secure the future of the Volt and if you want to be part of it, you can be."

Lexi looked at Deb. "Before you ask if you're chopped liver,

I have some ideas that could include both of us, but you're going to have to wait until I can attend meetings without looking like a boxer."

Matthew said, "I'm heading back to Kenya tomorrow. I know you said you probably couldn't forgive me, Lexi, but I hope we can stay in touch or maybe one day you'll come and see the work I do. Thank you for allowing me to be part of the adventure and into your life."

Nathan gave him a bear hug and as he let go, he handed him a check. "I sold the watch. You made me think when you said it could fund your clinic, so take it and go help save some more lives."

Matthew walked towards Lexi and reached out his hand. This time, she took it.

"Again, I'm so very sorry for what I did, please stay in touch."

Lexi looked at him and realized she was no longer seeing a ghost haunting her from the past. She was grateful he had come. "I'm not ready to use the F word, but I will work on it if you promise to work on forgiving yourself."

As Matthew closed the door behind him, Lexi said with enthusiasm, "Zander, let's talk about this date."

ACKNOWLEDGMENTS

I am grateful for everyone who has helped to bring my story to the page.

The pre-reading team who worked through the unedited version giving me their fabulous feedback.

Beth Lingard
Jennifer Reeves
Jessica Forbes

Ecologist: Barbara Albrecht, who fights to improve the quality of the environment and helps my running friends and I to identify the wildlife we see on our runs.

Book Coach: Jocelyn Lindsay, who encouraged me to keep going when I wanted to give up.

ABOUT THE AUTHOR

Trish Taylor was living and working in England, happily settled in her role as a career counselor and part-time jazz singer. An encounter with a Salsa-dancing American literally swept her off her feet. They married and moved to the United States where she changed direction, training in mindset coaching and alternative therapies. She began writing self-help books to aid her clients. She now writes, runs, birdwatches and talks to her cat. Trish lives in Florida with her husband.

This is her first book of fiction.

She is the author of a range of non-fiction books:

Put The Kettle On: An American's Guide to British Slang, Telly and Tea
Yes! You Are Good Enough: End Imposter Syndrome, Overthinking and Perfectionism and Live the Life YOU Want
Why Am I Scared? Face Your Fears and Learn to Let Them Go
I'm Never Drinking Again: Maybe It's Time to Think About Your Drinking?
A Brief Guide to the Magic of NLP: Neuro-Linguistic Programming for Everyday Life
Co-author with Eric Harvey. *Respect in the Workplace: You Have to Give It to Get It*

Connect at www.trishtaylorauthor.com.

www.ingramcontent.com/pod-product-compliance
Lightning Source LLC
Chambersburg PA
CBHW021131190726

48288CB00008B/2608